ELEMENTS OF CHEMISTRY

HEAT (PART 2)

PENNY REID

[1]
THERMOCHEMISTRY

I WALKED THROUGH the house and the partygoers in search of quiet, space, and cleanliness. In the end, numbness descended and I embraced it. Basically, I decided not to care, and instead thought about my ideal party.

Give me a small intimate gathering of five people, a dinner party, where one-on-one conversations can be had, where people talk about current events, good books, good food, and weird news. That was my idea of a good time.

Not keg stands with a hundred people on a private island, with a DJ and underage girls puking in the bushes while venereal diseases were shared in the hot tub. Add to that Martin ignoring me and making out with random girls.

Not that. That was not fun.

I happened upon the library, or a room with a lot of books. It was packed with people and I'm pretty sure a few someones copped a feel as I tried to squeeze past the bodies in favor of the books. I scanned the shelves and felt a spark of something good, something nice as I spotted *Twenty Years After,* by Alexandre Dumas. I'd been meaning to read it for a while. It was about the three musketeers twenty years after their initial adventures.

To my right someone threw up on the carpet. I glanced at the guy and decided that if people were throwing up on the carpet then no one would care if I borrowed a book.

I pulled it off the shelf, clutched it to my chest, and went in search of a quiet space. I roamed the house for a bit, thought about going back to the souped-up golf carts and just waiting for everyone outside, but dismissed the idea. The available reading light would be insufficient. I also dismissed the bedrooms, as those would be occupied. A bathroom was an obvious choice, but not a good one because they'd be in high demand, and it would be selfish of me to tie one up so I could read.

I tried to find a closet with a light. At one point I almost tripped over a passed-out Ben in the hallway. I glanced around and found Herc hovering nearby, talking to several girls. He gave me a nod. I returned it and continued on my way. I decided my suspicions were correct: Herc had been following Ben around. I wondered if Ben had inadvertently consumed his own date-rape drug.

I made a mental note to contact the campus police department about Ben when I got home. Martin had promised to handle it—whatever that meant—but if *handling it* meant no jail time for Ben, I would step in and do something.

Shaking off thoughts of Ben the rapist, I ended up stumbling upon the laundry room quite by accident. It was actually perfect. There was a clean comforter folded on the washer and plenty of reading light. Therefore, I arranged the blanket and hopped up on the machine, leant against the wall with the cushy comforter at my back, and began to read.

It was a truly excellent book. I didn't know how much time passed —two hours, maybe three. That Porthos...I swear, he's a riot. His antics always make me laugh. Although Athos was my favorite. I think it was because of his tragic past. I was a bit of a sucker for a guy with a tragic past.

"What are you doing?"

I lifted my eyes at the sound of Martin's voice, but not immediately. I finished the paragraph I was reading, then I looked up, holding my place in the book with my thumb.

He was dressed in swim trunks and he was wet, with beads of water dripping down his chest. As such, he looked super hot. However, only the right side of his body was visible as the door blocked the other side. His hand was still on the doorknob and he leaned a tad to one side, into the room.

My eyes wandered over his form and I allowed myself to appreciate the beauty of Martin Sandeke like I might admire the beauty of a cold, soulless statue. Physically, he was a magnificent male specimen: corded muscle, long limbs, and rigid angles. Even his temples were drool worthy, especially since I knew his head housed a giant—albeit mismanaged—brain. Truly, he was one of our finest. His ancestors should really give themselves a big pat on the back.

A little pool of water had gathered at his feet, which made me wonder how long he'd been standing in the doorway. My eyes traveled upward again and I noticed he wore an angry expression. He looked livid.

I started a little at the heated annoyance in his stare. Then I glanced around the laundry room, searching for the source of his anger. I found that I was still alone. Therefore, I surmised his fury must be directed at me.

But, just to be sure, I said, "Who? Me?"

"Yes. You," he growled, then stepped into the room and closed the door behind him. "What are you doing in here?"

I raised the book and tipped my head toward it. "I'm reading."

Martin exhaled loudly, another growl. "I can see that, Parker. But why the fuck are you in here reading?"

I frowned at his use of profanity, my shoulders bunching with tension. I realized I'd gotten used to it, how often he cussed; I'd accepted it as part of him. But that was before he'd left me standing at the entrance to a party I didn't want to attend, and that was before I'd seen him kissing a random girl.

"It's the first sequel to The Three Musketeers. I've been meaning to read it. I found it on the shelf in the library—or living room, or whatever room. There are too many rooms in this house, so I don't know what half of them are called."

Martin gritted his teeth, and I got the distinct impression he wanted to strangle me. "Parker. This is a party. And you're in the laundry room? Reading?"

I paused a beat to make sure this wasn't a trick question. When I could find nothing amiss with his interrogation, I nodded slowly. "Yes. This is a party. I am in the laundry room reading."

"Why? What is *wrong* with you?"

My mouth opened and closed but no words arrived, because his questions continued to confuse me. Finally, I admitted, "Martin, I don't know what you want me to say or why you appear to be upset. I found the book when I was in one of the several rooms with lots of books. I've been meaning to read it. So I picked it up and found a quiet place. Why are you so angry?"

He charged at me and I ineffectually scrambled backward on the washing machine. In less than two seconds he'd pulled the book from my hands, slapped it on the counter at my left, and braced his arms on either side of my legs, leaning forward.

I realized he'd made me lose my page in the book. I decided to ignore my urge to vocalize this complaint, because his eyes were beyond heated.

They were incensed blue flames. I braced myself, my gaze wide and watchful, and flinched when he lifted a hand. I relaxed a smidge when he used it to push my hair off my shoulder.

When he spoke, his voice was low, strained, like he was trying very hard to control his temper. "I brought you here as my date. That was our agreement."

I nodded once. "Yes. I know."

"And, instead of talking to people or having fun, you're in here reading a book."

I kept my voice even and calm, tried to sound soothing. "I am having fun. I'm reading a book."

"You're trying to punish me for winning our bet, for bringing you here."

I shook my head, hoping he would see the honesty in my denial. "I'm not. I promise. I like to read."

"Who comes to a party, an entire mansion at your disposal, and reads Dumas in a laundry room? I've been looking for you for two hours."

He's been looking for me? For two hours? Why would he do that?

"If you've been looking for me then why are you wet?"

"This place has pools with caves, and I've been through all of them searching for you. You're avoiding me."

"Honestly, Martin…" I shrugged. "I didn't think you'd notice."

"You didn't think I'd *notice*?" he roared.

I winced. "That's right."

He blinked at me once, then held perfectly still. His features completely motionless as though his face were stuck in angry suspension. I could see something building behind his eyes, like how you can see a far-off storm gathering in the distance. Therefore, I decided it would be best to explain before he lost control of his temper.

"Earlier, after I changed," I motioned quickly to the string bikini I was wearing, "I went back to the deck and saw you had your hands full —and at one point, your mouth full of a tongue that wasn't yours—so I figured you were good. You know, entertained, taken care of, no need of my escort services."

He flinched, blinked rapidly during my explanation like I'd splashed water in his face, and his back straightened.

"You saw that?" He appeared to be surprised.

Lifting my hands up between us like I surrendered, I nodded and continued, "But, no worries. I understand that kissing random girls is in your wheelhouse. Which, like I've been saying all along, is another reason why we're not compatible. Because, as I've said—and no judgment—I'm not really into kissing guys who kiss other girls. *That's* not in my wheelhouse. So you should go return to your women folk. I'll be down here reading; no rush. But if you plan on spending the night, let me know so I can ensure to hitch a ride with Eric and Sam, or Ray. For your own safety though, please make sure the sheets are clean. I overheard one of the guys in the library say that he thinks he has ringworm. I didn't ask which bedroom he used."

Martin's eyes narrowed as I spoke and his mouth curved into an unhappy line. When I was finished he lifted his gaze to the ceiling, subtly shaking his head; he paired an eye roll with a whispered, "Fuck."

Again, I flinched at the profanity and scrunched my nose, my gaze moving back to the discarded book. I wondered how much longer this conversation was going to take, because Porthos's shenanigans were seriously cracking me up.

"Parker..."

My eyes jumped back to his, which were now once again on me. He didn't look as angry, but he did look frustrated.

"Yes?"

Martin lifted his hand like he was going to put it on my leg, but stopped when I stiffened. He cursed again. Shook his head, again. Gritted his teeth, again.

"Look," he said, "if you'd stayed, then you would have seen me push her away. I'm not interested in her." His expression relaxed, and I saw the flash of hopeful vulnerability. My heart leapt in response.

Stupid heart.

He cupped my cheek, his thumb tracing the line of my jaw, and added, "I'm not interested in any girl here other than you."

I pressed my lips together to keep from frowning, though I knew my eyes betrayed my disbelief because Martin's frustration visibly spiked.

Before he could continue, I interjected, "Martin, even if I believed you—which I don't—it doesn't really matter. You pawned me off on Ray for the drive over. When we walked in here, into this house, you left me. You walked away from me, and you didn't introduce me to anyone. You went off as though I wasn't there. I don't know any of these people and I'm terrible at parties."

His gaze turned thunderous. "Is that what this is about? Are you down here because you're pissed that I left? I thought I was doing what you wanted. You said that you didn't want me to be possessive and hover. Is this some kind of punishment? Because I don't respond well to that kind of mind-fuckery or passive-aggressive bullshit."

Despite my desire to stay calm, his words felt like gasoline on a fire I'd been carrying around in my chest, but had thus far managed to keep under control. My temper rose and with it the volume of my voice.

"No, Martin. I don't do passive-aggressive and I don't punish people. That *is* one of my life rules. I'm honest. If something upsets me, I'll let you know. But in order for me to be upset, I'd have to be surprised by your terrible behavior. What you did, leaving me in a room full of strangers and giving CPR to female partygoers didn't upset me, because I don't really expect more from you."

It was his turn to flinch. He sucked in a sudden breath and straightened away from me, his eyes cooling to frigid icicles. "What the hell is that supposed to mean?"

"It means you're used to getting what you want or who you want when you want it. And I couldn't care less if you were upstairs, right now, having a ginormous orgy with the ringworm gang. Because I've known all along that you are a jerk-face and you don't know how to treat people with decency."

His mouth fell open, presumably at my words and my hostile tone, and he stared at me. His expression was that of someone who'd been stunned speechless.

I didn't like losing my temper. In fact, I prided myself on how laid-back and in control of my reactions I was, and how I never lost my temper. Therefore, this loss of control was another irritating new development since spending time with jerky Martin Sandeke.

At length, he found his voice. Though, surprisingly, he didn't sound quite as angry. "If you don't like how I treat you, then why do you keep letting me kiss you?"

"Opportunity and lust."

Gah…that was spiteful.

He flinched like I'd kicked him and he glanced away. His reaction made my heart hurt, and therefore, I heaved a gigantic regretful sigh.

My words came out in a rush. "That's not true. I'm sorry. I shouldn't have said that. The truth is…"

He lifted his eyes to mine, and the raw emotion made me forget myself. It made me forget to be cautious. Without really thinking about it or planning to do so, I gave him the whole embarrassing truth.

"You're smart—in fact, you have flashes of brilliance which is a huge turn on for me—and you're funny and charming when you want to be. And sometimes, you treat me with kindness and respect. Also, you're a good kisser. I thought at first it was my lack of experience, but now I think you're just an exceptionally good kisser. I like kissing you. I like the way it feels. I love how you make me feel when you touch me. But what feels good isn't always what's good for me, and I'm not willing to settle for being with someone who *sometimes* treats me well. I'd rather be alone."

With the end of my unplanned speech the numbness returned. I peered at him in a way I hoped demonstrated my acceptance of the situation and the impossibility of us, and I reached for my book. I did all this while I tried to suppress my blush of mortification. "Now, if you'll excuse me, Porthos is rather charming and I'd like to finish this chapter before leaving."

Martin's glare moved from me to the book. Before I understood his intention, he'd reached for the book, pulled it from me, and tossed it over his shoulder. I yelped my surprised unhappiness, but couldn't retrieve the novel because he'd stepped forward again, crowding my space. He gripped my waist and yanked me forward so he was between my legs, and my chest was against his.

My mind might have been numbed to him, but my pants weren't. I sucked in a sharp breath at the contact, everything tightening and twisting and bracing for his touch.

He stared at me for a long moment, during which—I'm ashamed to admit—my heart rate quadrupled and my body responded by pressing more fully against him. When he did speak, his voice was a growly and hostile whisper. "Listen to me for one fucking second, okay?"

I also whispered, but only because he was whispering, "Only if you stop using the F-word like you get paid royalties every time you say it."

"I'll fucking use whatever fucking word I want to fucking use whenever I fucking want to," he whispered back.

I shook my head and spoke mostly to the other washing machine and two dryers lining the walls. "Again, proving my point, jerk-face."

"Kaitlyn, you are irritating."

"Feeling is mutual, jerk-face."

"Especially when you're right."

"Well, you can..." I paused, blinked at him and his shocking words. "Wait, what?"

His eyes moved over my face as he spoke and the tension in his body eased. Peripherally, I noted he was wrapping his arms around me, one hand sliding under the string of my bikini and against my bare back.

"I'm sorry." He was still using his growly whisper.

I narrowed my eyes, attempting to peer into and through his words, looking for trickery. As well, I was trying to ignore the wave of goosebumps that had spread outward from where his hot palm pressed against my back, and the fluttering butterflies in my stomach.

A beautiful man is the devil's most potent weapon.

A few seconds ticked by while we stared at each other. I wondered if I looked as hostile as he did.

I responded, "Do you even know why you're apologizing?"

"Yes." Another growl.

"Why? Why are you apologizing?"

"Because I shouldn't have left you when we got here. I should have kept you close to me, and I shouldn't have let Danielle close enough to touch me, not when we're together."

My brain stumbled on the word *together*, and I frowned my confusion at his accurate listing of offenses. "This seems like a miraculously sudden apology."

His jaw flexed. "Are you seriously going to give me shit about apologizing?"

I shook my head. "No. No, I am not. I accept your apology. Thank you for apologizing."

His eyes flickered between mine, then lowered to my mouth. "Now it's your turn."

"My turn?"

"Your turn to apologize."

My eyebrows bounced an inch upward. "What am I apologizing for?"

"For always assuming I'm an asshole."

It was my turn to stare at him while he filled the silence, his chin dipping toward mine, our mouths scant inches apart.

"I didn't leave you because I was trying to be a jerk. I wanted to give you your space. I thought I'd circle back around and find you... prove that I trusted you. I don't know how to be near you without being possessive, because every time a guy looks at you I want to rip his head off. I've never come to a party with someone before. I don't know girl-rules. This is new for me. And I wasn't kissing Danielle. She kissed me and I pushed her away, but you obviously didn't stick around for the half second it took me to tell her I wasn't interested."

My mouth opened and closed. I was shocked. His words shocked me.

He wasn't finished. "You promised me you would give this a try. But you've already made up your mind about me. Sitting down here, avoiding me, isn't trying. Seeing another girl kiss me, and then walking away, isn't trying. Assuming the worst of me isn't trying. Either you do this for real, or you break your promise. But don't put this all on me. I'm not a fucking mind-reader."

I sputtered, perplexed. "Okay, I'm sorry. I'm sorry I assumed the worst. I shouldn't have done that."

"Apology accepted. Now kiss me."

I evaded his mouth by leaning to the side and bracing my palms against his chest. "Wait, just wait a minute. I don't know. What did you want me to do? Walk over and rip that girl's hair out?"

"Yes." He stated this emphatically and paired it with a single head nod, his eyes lowering to my breasts. The small triangles of the string bikini did very little to cover them; I felt like I was wearing pasties and floss. Martin seemed to both love it and hate it because he released a frustrated and distracted sounding sigh and lifted his gaze to mine. "Yes, if I matter to you, then yes."

"Martin...I'm..." I shook my head, having difficulty finding words. They were hiding in all the closets of my brain, the little bastards.

Finally I managed, "I'm not like that. I'm not going to enter a race I can't win."

His hand moved from the middle of my back to my waist, his thumb drawing a gentle circle on my ribs, tickling me, touching me, feeling me. "You totally could have taken her. She's not a good fighter. She favors her right side."

I laughed because what he said was preposterous and therefore funny, and I was relieved to see that even after our harsh exchange, he was trying to cut the tension with humor.

"That's not what I meant. I know I could have knocked her out. She probably hasn't eaten in days, the poor dear."

"Then what do you mean? Because you are the only boat in this regatta."

I shook my head, feeling high and low and everything in between. "I don't know how to do this. I'm the bow-out-gracefully kind of girl, not the brawling-for-my-man-at-a-party kind of girl. Not when my competition is a supermodel."

Martin's stare was severe and stern, and his thumb stilled on my skin. "If all I wanted was a supermodel then I wouldn't be here with you."

I scrunched my face at this. It sounded like a compliment, but it also sounded like an insult. I had no illusions I was supermodel material, but to my ears his statement emerged as, *If I wanted someone good-looking then I wouldn't be with you.* I knew that was wrong and unfair and twisting his words, so I threw that messed-up interpretation into the garbage where it belonged...but my sinking heart lingered.

He growled a sigh and rolled his eyes. "That's not...that came out wrong. What I mean is, yes—of course I want to be with someone who is beautiful. But you're so much more than that. Why would I bring a single scull to an eight-man race? I wouldn't."

"A single skull?"

"A scull. It's a boat with one rower and two oars. An eight-man racing shell would beat a single scull every time."

I squinted at him and nodded once, rolled my lips between my teeth, and tried not to laugh at his manly rowing analogy. I let him know I understood the gist of what he meant and that I wasn't going to hold the conversation hostage.

He continued, "But I need you to fight, not bow out gracefully. When you want something, you fight for it."

I lowered my eyes to his neck, watched him swallow. I inhaled and held the breath in my lungs, unsure what to say or how to proceed. This was not how I foresaw the discussion progressing.

"Look at me," he demanded, and I did.

"When you want something, you fight for it," he repeated, the pressure of his hands increasing on my body, telling me he wanted me, telling me he would fight for me.

Then he asked, "Do you want me?"

I stared at him for a beat, the answer having immediately formed in my brain, but I hesitated. I felt like admitting my want for him would give Martin power over me, power I wasn't ready to cede.

He must have seen my struggle because before I could speak, he volunteered, "You don't have to answer that right now. You tell me when you're ready, okay?"

I nodded, releasing an unsteady sigh. "Martin..."

"Shh, just...just listen to me." He licked his lips, his mouth scant inches from mine. His eyes told me he was interested and invested, the rest of his body communicating that everything he'd said was the truth. I might not have been a gazelle, but his body wanted my body.

Eventually he continued on a rumbly, seductive whisper, "Maybe you're right. Maybe I don't know how to treat people. But I meant it when I said that I...fucking hell, I want you. I like you. I'm all in. I'm not a liar and I'm doing my best here. You need to meet me part way."

I nodded, no longer feeling numb.

I read the intention in his eyes before he moved and I shivered in anticipation. He slid his hand from my ribs up to my neck and pulled the string holding my top up. He leaned just two inches away and the flimsy thing immediately acquiesced, the little triangles ineffectually supporting my D-cup fell, baring me.

"I need to touch you," he said even as he touched me, both of his hands sliding into place, massaging, kneading.

I sighed, arched my back, offering myself more fully to his wonderfully callused hands.

"I need you to touch me," I whispered on a gasp. His fingers tugged on my nipples, sending liquid fire straight to my core.

He bent his head, bit my neck, then gently kissed the two love bites he'd left yesterday. "I like these. I like seeing my mark on you."

He used his knuckles, brushing them back and forth over the tight peaks. I tried to press myself tighter against him, needing his palms, not the light, maddening, teasing sweeps of the back of his hands.

He tongued my ear, making me tremble, before his hot exhale spilled against my jaw and neck. "I want to taste you."

I had a flash, a thought, an image pass through my mind and it made me groan. Martin, bending over me, kneeling, his mouth at my center, licking, sipping, tasting, sucking, as I reclined on the washing machine and his blue eyes watched me. Some dark, pleasure-seeking part of myself became obsessed with this idea.

"Oh, please do," I panted. Obviously the time for pride was at an end.

He chuckled. It sounded wicked, throaty, and really evil. Unsurprisingly, wicked and evil were really hot on Martin Sandeke. Desperate for what my body wanted, I brushed my fingertips down the front of his chest, lower to his abdomen, and lower still into the material of his swimsuit.

He sucked in a stunned breath and I felt his muscles tighten, grow rigid as I cupped his length, gripped it. The feel of it, the hardness, the thickness thrilled me. It was the greediest part of him and a surge of aroused power made my sex pulse.

"Fuck me," he exhaled, his eyes closing, his hips moving in an inelegant, wild movement.

"Surprised?" I asked. I was surprised. I was surprised by my vixenish boldness.

He laughed, it was tight and tortured sounding. "You have to stop," he said even as he pressed himself more completely in my hand.

"Or what?"

"Or I'm going to come all over your tits."

I thought about that. I'd seen something similar in a porno last year. At the time I'd cringed, somewhat grossed out. But with Martin it sounded really sexy. I didn't see a problem.

"Okay."

"Don't say it unless you mean it." He looked wild, feral, and I knew he was trying to control some dark impulse to take without asking.

"I mean it."

He growled, then covered my mouth with his, devoured me—his lips and tongue bruising, desperate, almost angry. He pushed his swim shorts down then moved one of his hands to cover mine where I held him. Guiding me, he gave himself a rough stroke. I felt him shudder, his mouth separating from mine as he inhaled a shaky breath.

"Fuck, fuck, fuck..." he said.

"Say my name," I whispered. The constant *fucks* were seriously getting on my nerves. Therefore I thought I'd offer him an alternative. "Say Kaitlyn instead."

His eyes flashed. Hips grinding into my palm, jaw clenched, he growled, "Kaitlyn."

I smiled. My smile made him groan. His head fell against my shoulder and his hands grabbed fistfuls of my bottom. He chanted, "Kaitlyn, Kaitlyn, Kaitlyn..." and, honestly, it got me hot. Soon I was panting.

One of his hands released me and returned to my breast, giving it rough treatment, grabbing and pinching while he bit my shoulder with his sharp teeth and thrust into my hand.

"Oh God, Kaitlyn." The words were tight yet uncontrolled. Every one of his muscles strained, flexed. His hands on my body tightened, his grip so hard I wondered if he'd leave bruises, and I finally under-stood what people meant when they said, *Come apart in my hands.*

Because Martin came apart in my hands. He came apart all over me, and yes, part of the coming apart landed on my breasts. Basically he came apart on everything but my hand. I gasped, not at all prepared, then laughed my surprise.

Sure, I'd seen pornos and money shots. But Martin's semen seemed to launch out of him—and there was a great deal more of it than what I'd seen in the dirty films.

His breathing was ragged and he sagged against me, his grip now loose, the tremors receding and leaving him gasping. I brought my other hand up to his back and stroked him from his shoulder blades to the base of his spine, then back again. I felt and heard him sigh. It sounded content. I did it again and again, soothing him.

He placed a kiss on my shoulder, lingered there as his heart slowed.

"I didn't know it was going to do that," I said suddenly, voicing my thoughts.

He stiffened—not much, just a little—and leaned just far enough away to bring my eyes into focus.

"You didn't know what was going to do what?"

"Your..." I hesitated, feeling unaccountably embarrassed. It was strange, I didn't mind doing it, but talking about it made me feel squeamish and uncomfortable. I cleared my throat, determined to soldier on and not be a ninny. So I said bravely, "I didn't know your ejaculate was going to shoot out like that."

His eyebrows jumped and he gave me a surprised, crooked smile. "My ejaculate?"

"Yes. Like a cannon blast of semen, and there was—is—a lot of it. It's everywhere."

Martin gave a surprised laugh, looking at me like I was weird and wonderful.

But then he sobered suddenly and asked, "Are you...are you uncomfortable?" He shifted like he was going to grab one of the washcloths folded neatly on the dryer.

"No. Not particularly. But it's getting a little cold."

He stared at me. I stared back. I didn't know what I was supposed to do, how to let his penis go, because my hand was still around it. So I tried stroking him again. He winced, jumped away, and gulped air.

"Kaitlyn, no, no, don't do that."

15

"Sorry. I didn't...I mean, I don't know what to do after..."

He exhaled, placed his hands on his hips, and dropped his chin to his chest, but not before I saw his small smile.

Meanwhile, I did what I think anyone would do in my situation. I leaned back on the washing machine and gave him a good once-over because Martin Sandeke was naked. He was completely naked. And he was crazy beautiful. I'm not an idiot, so of course I was going to exploit this moment.

I sighed then bit my lip, because I was still aroused and he was naked. This was more pre-bedtime imagery for the win.

He lifted his head at the sound, his eyes moving over my body with what felt like a hungry compulsion. He must've noticed me doing the same because he smirked. Martin sauntered forward, grabbed a washcloth and wiped off my stomach and chest, taking more time and care than necessary.

At some point during his careful ministrations I began to feel inhibited—not because I was ashamed of my body—because I wasn't used to being on display. I wasn't used to being looked at while naked, with desire or otherwise. I'd always been modest, and therefore, as he tossed the dirty washcloth to the floor I moved to cover myself.

Martin intercepted, then covered my hands with his, halting my progress.

"What are you doing?"

"I'm covering up."

"Why?"

"Because..." I glanced around the room, feeling oddly embarrassed, then answered with simple honesty, "Because I'm not used to this, to being exposed like this."

Martin released my hand and I finished tying the strap, but then he slipped his fingers into the cup of my bikini and massaged, caressed, possessed—almost like he was communicating that it didn't matter whether I covered myself. My body was his to touch how he liked. This was confusing because it thrilled me. I felt dominated and I liked it. He loomed, hovering, peering down at me, all tall and strong and powerful...and naked.

"You have the most luscious breasts." He whispered this, then nipped at my lips, his tongue darting out to taste them.

"Oh? The most?" I panted.

I felt his smirk return. "Yes. The most."

"Luscious?"

"And delicious."

"Really? Are they flavored?"

"Yes. Kaitlyn flavored…and now Martin flavored. I wonder what the rest of you tastes like."

My eyes flickered to the door behind him as sounds of partygoers being loud and ruckusy ebbed and flowed, cutting through this little world we'd created in the laundry room. I gathered a deep breath, swallowing down my desire. I'd already ventured quite far out of my comfort zone for one night. I needed time to think and regroup.

So I shook my head, returning my eyes to Martin's. "No, no. I'm good."

He lifted a single eyebrow, clearly surprised. "You're…good?"

I nodded. "Yeah. That was fun…watching you and, um, touching you during. I'm good."

He studied me, his eyes narrowing. "What if I'm not good?"

I glanced to one side, then the other, trying to figure out why he wouldn't be good. "Did I not do it right?"

"No, no. Not at all. You did great. That's not what I meant. What if…" He paused, his eyes moving down the length of me, blazing a path that left goosebumps in its wake. He reached for my hand and brought my middle finger to his mouth. I was transfixed as he sucked it into his mouth, his tongue swirling. I moaned. I did. Because the inside of his mouth felt like the gateway to heaven.

"Oh, Martin, what are you doing?"

He withdrew my finger and rubbed the pad of it back and forth over his bottom lip. "I need to taste you, Kaitlyn. I want to fuck you with my tongue."

I shivered convulsively and had no idea how to respond to that, so I said, "I have no idea how to respond to that."

"Say yes. Say: Yes, Martin. I want you to fuck me…with your tongue."

"I don't think my mouth can say those words out loud. I'm not that outgoing."

He grinned, bringing my knuckles to his mouth and slipping the aforementioned tongue against the back of my middle and index finger, licking the space between them where they joined. I gasped because the spot seemed to be a wormhole; he'd bent time and space creating a shortcut to my clitoris.

I yanked my hand away, hopped off the machine, abruptly standing, forcing him to take a step back. He moved to reach for me but I placed two hands on his chest—*stupid perfect chest*—holding him at bay.

"Just…just give me a minute."

"Kaitlyn—"

"No, no, no. I need a minute."

"Let me—"

"I don't think I'm ready for that, okay?"

He caged me in, his hands on the machine behind me. "You seemed ready for it earlier." His voice was teasing, held sensual promise that my pants really liked. I think my pants are the president of the Martin Sandeke sensual promise fan club.

I shook my head, staring up at him, my words rushing out of me. "I wasn't. I mean, I wanted to and I want you to, but I don't think I'm ready…yet. I mean I just had my first orgasm yesterday afternoon. We just kissed for the first time on Friday. *Friday*. I can't move this fast. I need time to acclimate to changes, process what they mean."

His scorching gaze subdued, grew thoughtful, and he straightened, giving me space.

I continued, "If I keep giving in while we're in the moment then none of this has meaning."

This last statement seemed to make a huge difference. He rocked back on his feet then took two steps away; to my surprise, he was nodding. "That makes sense."

I clasped my hands and returned his nod. "It does, right? I mean, we could jump each other's bones now, in this laundry room, but what would it really mean? It would feel good—really, really good—but—"

"But it wouldn't have meaning for you," he finished for me, his eyes searching mine. Martin's voice deepened and his gaze grew open and earnest. "I want it to have meaning, Parker. And I'm fine with waiting for some things, but I still need to touch you."

I gave him a little smile, my hands on my hips. I felt a tad silly standing in front of him, talking about giving meaning to physical intimacy while the barest remnants of his sperm dried on my stomach and chest.

"And I still need you to touch me, Martin. That's part of this whole dating thing…I think. The point is, we're trying to figure it out, right? And I think we can."

"Good." He rushed forward, like he needed to be close. His hands moved to touch my waist, stalled, then settled benignly on my shoulders. "Good. We're on the same page."

"Good." I grinned, feeling excited.

It was, I realized, the first time I'd truly entertained the possibility that things might actually work between us. Before this moment I'd kept my guard up, trying to prove the null hypothesis, ready for Martin to mess up or for him to realize his interest in me was transitory and misplaced.

He must've seen some shift in my expression because his answering smile was soft and hopeful.

He asked, "You want to have some tacos?"

"What? Here? Now? They have tacos?"

"Yeah." Martin's eyes skated over my face and they lit at my delight. "They have a taco bar."

"Oh my God." I stared at him for a beat, my mouth agape, then nodded vehemently and declared, "Best party ever!"

[2]
CHEMISTRY OF THE ENVIRONMENT

I WOKE UP the next morning struck by a sudden idea of super genius.

Actually, it was almost noon when I woke up, so I guess I woke up the next afternoon struck by a sudden idea of super genius.

It had to do with something Martin had said the night before, just before we'd eaten our tacos.

Last night, after Martin grabbed a clean beach towel from the dryer, we left the laundry room of sensual promise. We held hands as we navigated the party; navigating the party with Martin was quite different than navigating it on my own. The sea of bodies parted— people catching sight of him or sensing him, all moved out of his way.

He steered us back to the deck, then continued his hasty strides toward the pool. Along one of the walls were three outdoor shower stalls. Martin turned on a shower, set the temperature to warm, and pulled me under with him, rinsing the last of our encounter from our skin.

This left me feeling both cleaner and dirtier. Cleaner for obvious reasons. Dirtier, because he made no attempt to school his expression as he looked at me. Clearly, he appreciated my form; his eyes followed the trail of water as it flowed over my shoulders, between my breasts, down my stomach and legs. Under the burden of his scorching gaze, I attempted to remind myself of my feminist ideals, that I was not put on this earth to be attractive to men.

But those ideals felt really faraway, maybe a little naïve, and a lot inconvenient.

Being desired and desirable was a heady feeling. It was addictive; it felt really, really good. And the way Martin looked at me and desired me, with forceful concentration and barely restrained intensity, made me wonder if Oreos and yoga pants were all that great after all.

That thought felt like sacrilege.

Then he bent and whispered in my ear, "All I can think about is touching you."

At the time, the comment made me hot all over because all I could think about was Martin touching me.

But in the clear light of early afternoon it made me realize that the touching—though verra verra nice—might actually be the problem.

Sam was, once again, sleeping in the bed with me. I'd tried to explain what had happened with Martin at the party, the PG version, and how we'd misinterpreted the kiss. She interrupted my explanation to tell me she already knew we'd misinterpreted the kiss. Apparently Sam had taken it upon herself at the party to confront the leggy blonde, Danielle, on my behalf. Danielle admitted that Martin wasn't interested. Sam then spent most of the night trying to find me to tell me the news.

Once she spotted me eating tacos with Martin she figured he'd found me and we'd worked it out.

However, Sam made it a point to insist that she and I sleep together. I think, in a way, we'd become each other's chastity belts. If we were sleeping with each other then we couldn't be doing more than sleeping with anyone else.

I left the bed quietly, showered, changed into shorts and a T-shirt, then went in search of Martin. I found Ray and Griffin first. They were on the multi-level balcony that ran the length of the back of the house. To my surprise, they were studying.

Ray informed me that Martin might not be up yet as it was one of the only mornings they'd planned not to practice.

"He tries to sleep in for as long as possible if there's no practice," Ray explained. "But I can tell you where his room is. I don't think he'd mind if you woke him up."

"Hmm…" I hesitated. I didn't want to interrupt his sleep, especially if he rarely had an opportunity to sleep in.

"I don't think he'd mind at all," Griffin added with a dimpled grin, his brown eyes moving in slow appraisal from my ankles to my eyes.

I gave him a narrowed glare. He looked like the type to eat lo mein leftovers if given the opportunity.

"Sure, okay," I said to Ray. "Can you draw me a map?"

While Ray pulled out a blank piece of paper to draw a diagram of the house, Griffin returned my suspicious gaze with a teasing twist of his lips.

"So your grandfather is an astronaut?"

I nodded. "Yep."

"And your mom, she's the senator, right?"

"That's right."

"Didn't your grandma work on the atomic bomb, or something?"

"Something like that." My maternal grandmother was a physicist. She didn't work directly on the Manhattan project, but she did help the US government equip the earliest nuclear submarines.

"Must be weird coming from such a famous family."

I wrinkled my nose. "We're not famous."

"That's not true. You're like American royalty. Isn't your dad the president of something?"

"No. He's a dean at a college of medicine."

Griffin blew out a low whistle, his gaze growing less appraising and more introspective. He sat up straighter, his face and tone becoming serious, almost reverent. "So, you're like really smart then, right? What are you going to do? What's your major? You'll probably cure cancer or something."

I stared at him for a beat, not wanting to respond. I was proud of my family, but their accomplishments were not my accomplishments, their ambitions were not my ambitions.

For better or for worse, our ceiling and our floor are initially judged by our ancestry. People expected me to reach for the stars.

I was smart, but I wasn't a genius physicist working on nuclear submarines, or an astronaut, or the dean of a college of medicine. I didn't have the drive for greatness. I lacked the patience required for that kind of pressure. I had the drive for normalcy and anonymity and playing around on my guitar.

I shifted my gaze to Ray's and found him watching me, his eyebrows suspended over his eyes, as though to say, *See. You're the ultimate marriage girl.*

I ignored Griffin's question, giving him a tight, noncommittal smile, then affixed my attention to Ray. "So, Ray, how close are you to being done with that map?"

* * *

MARTIN WAS ASLEEP when I found him. He was shirtless, all tangled up in his simple brown sheets and comforter on a twin bed that looked too small for him. He held a pillow to his chest, another was at his back, and another under his head. The twin bed was pushed against a corner; he'd surrounded himself on all sides with cushy comfort, like he was being embraced while he slept.

The size of the bed surprised me. I was also surprised by how small his room was. It was maybe double the size of just the king bed I'd been sleeping in and was sparsely furnished, like a real bedroom might be. In addition to the twin bed, there was a dresser with no mirror, a desk with a simple wood chair, and a side table. Stuff littered the surfaces like a person really lived here.

It was the opposite of the palatial suite he'd put me in. My room was a fantasy of sterile white and luxury, the kind of room you'd see in a fancy magazine. His was cozy, messy, and real. It reminded me of my room at my parents' house.

I watched him sleep for a full minute, hovering at the entrance to the room like a creeper. This thought made me smile. Instead of being a hovering, indecisive creeper, I decided to close the door behind me and sit at his desk, be a full-fledged lurking creeper instead, maybe give him a little fright when he woke up and found me staring at him. This thought made me laugh with sinister glee.

I pulled out the chair and was just arranging myself when Martin scared the crap out of me. He sat up, grabbed me, pulled me into his arms, and brought me to the bed. He then rolled me under him and pinned me to the mattress.

"Ohmygod, Martin!" The wind was driven from my lungs by fright. "You scared me!"

He was planking on the mattress, his eyes piercing yet laughing, touching me only where his hands held my wrists above my head. "Good morning, Parker."

"How long have you been up?" I scowled at him, willing my heart to calm and the brief spike of adrenaline to recede.

"For about five minutes. I was up when you knocked and I heard the door open." He grinned down at me. His voice was deliciously roughened by sleep.

"Do you always grab girls and throw them on your bed when you wake up?"

"Only if that girl is Kaitlyn Parker."

I appreciated that he'd just used my own line against me and I shook my head at his shenanigans. This seemed to make him happy because his eyes lit with menacing satisfaction.

But then the longer we stared at each other the thicker the air grew between us, and the more difficult it became for me to breathe. His gaze also changed and lit with a new flame, both ominous and hungry. I momentarily forgot why I was there and what my super genius idea had been. All I knew was that his look held the promise of something that was going to feel fantastic.

"I like you here," he whispered, his eyes half lidded as they moved to my mouth, lingered there.

"You like me where?"

"In my bed. Being in my bed every morning should be one of your life rules."

"Oh…" Every inhale felt painful, tight.

"All I can think about is touching you," he said, lowering himself to kiss me.

It was the key phrase and it sparked my memory. I remembered why I was there. I remembered my super genius idea.

"Wait!" I said, turning my face to the side.

"Wait?"

"Yes, wait. I have an idea and it involves you not kissing me."

"That sounds like a terrible idea." He nuzzled my neck, licking my throat, using his hot breath to make me squirm.

"It also involves you letting me go."

"Another terrible idea."

"But it's not. It's really genius…oh!"

Martin nudged my legs apart with his knee then settled himself on top of me, grinding his *good morning* wood into my center.

"You are so sweet," he said, biting me then tasting me with his tongue. "I can't get enough of you. I dreamt about you last night, under the shower—"

"Seriously, listen to me." My words were weak and I'd closed my eyes so I could focus on all the sensations associated with Martin above me, Martin licking me, Martin touching me. Instinctively I tilted my hips to cradle him. "This is really important and I think it'll…oh… oh, that feels good…"

His laugh was rumbly and pleased. "Are you going to give in, Kaitlyn? Do I get to taste your sweet pussy? Or should I make you come like this?"

"No." I shook my head, squeezing my eyes shut, my words breathless. "No. I want all of this to matter. I want it to last."

Martin stilled his movements, his mouth on my throat ceasing its exploration, and I felt his lithe body stiffen briefly, then relax.

"Ah…damn." He sighed, placing a soft, closed-mouth kiss to my collarbone then rolling to the side, releasing my wrists.

I pulled in a huge breath, filling my lungs with cool air, and pressed my knees together. My pants hated me. Hated. Me.

Damn was right.

Darn, damn, dammit, shoot, gosh darn it, heck.

We lay next to each other for a full minute. Our bodies touched, but we weren't actively touching each other. Our breathing similar degrees of harsh and ragged. I covered my face with my hands and found it flushed. I was not surprised. I felt hot all over.

"Martin…" My palms muffled my words, but I had to keep my hands on my face. If I didn't I might jump him and demand he provide my pants with satisfaction. "My super genius idea is as follows: I think we should institute No-Touch Tuesdays."

He said nothing for a long time, so long in fact, I wondered whether or not he'd heard me. I was about to repeat myself when I felt him shift so he was lying on his side. I glanced at him from between my fingers, found him leaning on his elbow, his head propped in one hand, his face contorted in horror.

"I don't think that's a good idea." He placed his other hand on my stomach, slipping his fingers under the hem of my shirt to connect with my bare skin as though to emphasize his words.

"Let me explain."

"Let me see your face."

"Fine." I hesitated then drew my fingers away, folding them over my chest. "Here is what I am thinking. Neither of us have ever really dated someone before, correct?"

He squinted at me. "I thought you said you had a boyfriend."

"He was gay."

Martin frowned. "What? How is that possible?" His eyes swept down, then up, then down, then up my body. Again, he looked horrified.

"It's not like I can turn a person gay. Obviously he was gay before we got together. He…well, I was his beard."

"And you went along with that?"

"No. I didn't know."

He studied me, his eyes searching. "How long were you together?"

"Four years."

"And you didn't know?"

"No. I didn't. I guess I had a very Disney-like perspective of dating before college, very neutered and naïve. We kissed, mostly at parties in front of other people. We held hands, hugged. But when we were together we hung out, had a good time. We were good friends. This is consistent with my parents' relationship. They love each other, but they're good friends first and foremost. I can count the number of times I've seen them kiss on one hand."

"You didn't want…I mean, didn't you want…"

"More? Yes. I did."

"And he…?"

"He said he wanted to wait until he was married."

"Why didn't you break up with him?"

I opened my mouth to respond, but then snapped it shut. I thought about Martin's question. I mulled it over for close to a minute.

Then I responded with the truth. "I don't know. I guess I thought… I don't know. It made sense at the time. We were good friends. We liked each other. We supported each other through a lot. I was there for him when his parents divorced and later when his father died of cancer. I was thirteen when we got together. We were Kaitlyn and Carter. People just expected us to be a unit."

"So you never did anything but kiss? For four years?"

I nodded.

He whistled out a breath from between his teeth, his eyes losing focus as they moved to a spot on the bed over my shoulder. "No wonder you need time…what an asshole."

I huffed a laugh. "He's a nice guy. He was just confused and I'm glad I could be there for him."

Martin's gaze moved back to mine and it sharpened as he frowned. "No. He's an asshole. He used you, he messed you up, made you think there was something wrong with you, that you aren't sexy, that you aren't goddamn gorgeous and fucking hot as hell. If he was a nice guy he would have broken things off so you could get felt up in the back of a car by someone who thought about nothing else but getting in your pants."

I wrinkled my nose at him. "That sounds delightful. I'm so sorry I missed out on some horny teenager using me to get his jollies."

"You mistake my meaning. I'm not talking about someone who was going to use you, who just wanted a warm body. You're too smart for that. You would've spotted a user a mile away. I'm talking about the guy who wouldn't have been able to stop thinking about *you,* because he wanted *you,* not some indiscriminate jerkoff."

"My purpose on this earth is not to be desirable to a man." The words slipped out of my mouth, the thought second nature.

Martin reared his head back and he stared at me—nay, he glowered at me—for several seconds. "What the hell does that mean?"

I shrugged, trying to think how to explain something so obvious to me. "It means I don't care if I'm desirable or not."

"That's bullshit. I call bullshit." Martin pressed his lips together and shook his head. The look he gave me made me laugh. It was so ridiculous on his face; like *Giiiiiirl, you crazy!*

"It's not bullshit!" I insisted through my laughter. "I don't want my decisions to be about what will make me more appealing to the opposite sex. I want my decisions to be about making a difference, being a good person."

"You do care," he said flatly. "Everyone cares. Every single person on his earth wants to be desired, wants to be wanted."

"Okay, let me rephrase then. I don't want to care. I strive to *not* care."

"Now that's something different," he conceded, his hand on my stomach moving lower, his fingers touching the skin just below my belly button as though feeling my skin were compulsory for him. "But don't you think it's about balance? And finding someone who... someone where it's good *to* care? Where their opinion matters because they matter? And being desired by that person, striving to be more desirable to that person, makes you better?"

Now it was my turn to stare at him. I didn't glower, though. I stared. His words were deep, verging on philosophical, a complete shock and a total turn on coming from this guy I'd labeled as a jerk-face.

"Martin Sandeke," I shook my head, my lips parted in surprise, "I was wrong about you. I'm sorry."

He grimaced. It was subtle, but it happened, and he glanced away toward the ceiling. "I don't know if you were wrong about me so much as the fact that everyone I've ever met in my entire life—before you— pissed me off."

I couldn't help it. I laughed again.

His eyes slid back to me and I saw a reluctant smile curve over his lips.

"Everyone?" I asked, teasing him and poking him in the ribs for emphasis.

"Not everyone, just most people. I don't like being framed by other people's expectations. Growing up, I was public property to my parents."

"Even your mother?"

"Especially my mother." He rolled his eyes and the tilt of his chin was resentful. "She wanted to be loved by everyone, but no one in particular. She wanted to be worshipped, but didn't care if people knew her."

"She was an actress, right?"

"Yes." He nodded once, his eyes going back to the ceiling. Martin flopped on his back next to me; his hand searched for mine, found it, brought it up so he could see it, and held it between both of his. "She died when I was thirteen."

"I'm sorry."

"Don't be. It was a relief."

"God, Martin." His callous remark sent the wind from my lungs. I drew myself up so I could look at his face. "That's a terrible thing to say."

"It's the truth. She was a user, an addict. She used me for publicity and stupid stuff all the time. She tried to get me into show business, modeling. I hated it. I didn't want to do it. She did...other things." Suddenly, he heaved a frustrated sigh. "I...I don't want to talk about this."

I pulled my hand free and draped my arm over him, laying my head on his shoulder, and gave him a squeeze. "Then we don't have to talk about this."

He gripped my arm, pressed it to his chest. "It's depressing, and I don't want to associate lying in my bed with you with depressing stuff. I want to associate it with hot, sweaty, naked stuff."

Despite the gravity of our conversation, his comment sent a wave of awareness through my body. I was amazed at how quickly, with just a few words, he was able to get me fired up.

"Well, we're not doing that today. Today is No-Touch Tuesday."

"We're touching now."

"You know what I mean. We're going to do fun stuff."

"I thought you said we weren't going to touch."

I smacked his shoulder. "We can do fun stuff that doesn't involve touching."

"Can you touch yourself? I don't mind watching."

That comment deserved a pinch. I lifted my head, leaned over him, and I pinched the skin of his ribs below his pectoral.

"Ow!" His hands flew to the spot where I'd assaulted him.

"That's what you get for your sass."

"Holy crap, Parker! That hurt. Fine. What did you have in mind?" I saw that he was rubbing his skin; his tone and expression were those of a petulant adolescent, though he looked like he was fighting a grin.

"I'm going to teach you how to dance and you're going to teach me how to row."

"I thought you didn't know how to dance?"

"I know how to ballroom dance. I'm going to teach you the tango."

He lifted an eyebrow; it was an eyebrow of suspicion. "You know how to tango?"

"I do."

"Hmm."

"And you'll teach me how to row."

"Hmm...I'll have to touch you to teach you."

31

"That kind of touching is fine, it's instructional touching. It's not done with carnal intentions."

"Parker, every time I touch you it's with carnal intentions." His voice was flat and his eyebrows arched.

I huffed and was proud of myself that I didn't roll my eyes or smile. "Well, you'll have to learn to control yourself for one day."

"Why are we doing this again? Why is this a good idea?" His eyes lowered to my breasts where they were pressed against his shoulder.

"Because we don't really know each other."

"I do know you."

I ignored this statement because it was nonsense. "We agreed last night that we want this to last, yes? Beyond this week?"

He nodded, distracted, still looking at my boobs.

"Gah…are you listening to me?"

"Yes. You want me to last."

I pinched him again.

He jumped. His eyes lifted to mine, and he grabbed my hands. "Stop pinching me."

"Stop being a horndog."

He tried to hold it together, but in the end he lost his battle with laughter. "You are so easy to tease."

"Oh? You want me to tease you back? 'Cause I can tease you back." My voice held a threatening edge, low and laced with threatening intent; it made me proud.

He stopped laughing. His eyes grew wide and sober. "Parker…"

"I think I still have that string bikini somewhere. Maybe I could help out by lathering up and washing the golf carts…"

He sighed—more like a growl—and his eyes shut. He released my wrists and pressed the base of his palms into his eye sockets. "That's not nice."

It was the first time I'd used my sexuality for anything…ever. I was so used to relying solely on my brain. Exploiting my femininity was kind of fun. *Who knew?*

Of course, this thought was immediately followed by guilt. My guilt reminded me that the generations before me—like my mother—

had worked tirelessly to free women from the bonds of sexuality as the primary source of female importance.

Women were more than the status of their hymen or their dress size.

Then my sexuality bitch-slapped my guilt. Then my guilt sucker-punched my sexuality. I mentally took a step back, leaving them to fight it out amongst themselves, like a giant squid and a sperm whale in the depths of the ocean.

I shook my head before I spoke, trying to disentangle myself from my dichotomous thoughts. "Then listen to me and stop teasing. If you actually want a relationship with someone you need to know them, and not just physically. No-Touch Tuesday is a good thing. It will give us some no-pressure time to find out more about each other."

"I know you." His eyes were still closed and he said this to the room.

"No. You don't. What do I like on my pizza?"

Martin was silent. I took this as a good sign. But he also looked despondent when his eyes opened and tangled with mine.

Obviously I needed to remind him that No-Touch Tuesday wasn't going to last forever.

"And then tomorrow…" I trailed my fingers down his chest, stomach, to the waistband of his boxers. He caught my wrist before I could slip my fingers inside.

"And then tomorrow, what?" he growled, his eyes glinting with a dangerous edge.

"And then tomorrow is Wednesday. Maybe we could play chess, or work on our chemistry assignment."

He shook his head slowly, his voice low and thick. "I don't think you understand how badly I want you."

Again, another wave of awareness spread through my body, sending pinpricks of sensation everywhere, but especially to my pants. Reflexively I clenched my thighs together.

"Martin—"

He sat up and bent forward, the movement silencing me, so that I lay back; basically we switched positions and he was hovering over me.

He held my gaze until the last possible second as he leaned forward and whispered, "So many ways..." He kissed my cheek, his hand gliding down my stomach, his fingers pushing into the band of my cotton shorts and teasing my curls, petting them, petting me. I tilted my hips, a visceral reaction to his touch; but I knew in my heart I needed to keep things from escalating.

"It's No-Touch Tuesday, Martin," I breathed, reaching for his wrist.

His hand stilled, and his face fell to my neck. "Fine. No-Touch Tuesday. But then tomorrow is going to be Wet-and-Wild Wednesday, and the next day will be Tongue-and-Teeth Thursday, and Friday..." He bit me, his teeth sharp—*why were his teeth so sharp?!*—then licked the spot. "Well, I think you can guess what's going to happen on Friday."

[3]

AQUEOUS EQUILIBRIUM CONSTANTS

No-Touch Tuesday was a huge success and a huge literal pain in my gluteus maximus.

I'd only been going over the basics of the tango for ten minutes when Eric and Sam caught us in the act. Our twosome became a foursome and this was a good thing, because the tango is not a dance for platonic, getting-to-know-you discussions. I showed Martin the correct hold position and he looked at me like he hated me a little.

Therefore, I paired with Eric, Sam paired with Martin, and at one point, Martin paired with Eric and tried to dip him.

Seeing Martin's silly side with his friend was a huge revelation. Also revealing was that he couldn't dance without taking over, even when he didn't know the steps very well. He could not cede control. He was incapable of allowing anyone else even a short period of leading. But he was also a fast learner and surprisingly graceful, and was soon taking Sam around the room with sure steps.

...typical. He's good at everything, except maybe being nice.

Rosa announced lunch on the balcony and I was starving. The four of us joined a few of the others and sat on the highest level, overlooking the ocean. Notably, Ben the rapist was absent. As was Herc.

Apparently they'd both stayed the night at the party and hadn't yet returned.

When the rest of the guys heard my plan to learn how to row, it was met with overwhelming excitement and enthusiasm. Though they didn't know me very well, it appeared rowers are always trying to convert other people into becoming rowers. As such, the group decided to take one of the boats out. Since two people were missing, Sam was drafted to replace Ben.

They also decided to take out a wooden boat—an antique they called Pocock—instead of the sleek carbon fiber Vespoli typically used for practice. Eric explained it would be easier to "set"—i.e. balance—with two new rowers as it was much bigger and didn't sit so high in the water.

They walked it out from the beach until the water reached their hips. Sam and I were too short to be much help with the boat because they carried it over their heads; therefore we brought out the oars.

Martin instructed me how to "rig" my oar, making sure the oar lock was completely fastened, then took me through the motions of rowing with just my arms—the catch, the sweep, the release, the return—making sure I said the words legs, body, arms; arms, body, legs as I moved. He also stood behind me, his arms around me, as we… *ahem* stroked.

O.o

"Rowing is about physics, specifically torque. It's about getting the most out of each stroke," he explained, whispering into my ear. His bare chest was at my back, his legs brushing against mine in the water. He made the act of rowing sound like a dirty, wonderful thing.

"How come you didn't teach me like that?" Ray asked. Both Martin and I turned toward Ray where he stood in the water by five-seat position. He lifted his chin and indicated to how Martin held me in his arms. "Why didn't you hold me like that?"

"Because you've got that rash," Martin said, completely deadpan.

"Oh…yeah. That's right." Ray nodded, chuckling. "Good point."

Once the guys felt sure we had the full motion of the stroke committed to muscle memory, they put us in the boat. I sat in Martin's seat—seat eight, the stroke seat at the stern—and Sam sat at the bow in seat one. We placed our feet in the shoes, stretchers is what they called them, and practiced rowing and balancing, sliding the seat, moving through the catch to release to return.

The guys held the boat in place and kept it level until Sam and I got used to being in the water on such a narrow craft. Then, when I was sure I had everything mostly right, Martin taught me how to feather my oar.

"Like this," he said as he showed me how he twisted his wrists, making the blade of the oar perpendicular to the water at the catch and sweep, but then after the release and during the return he instructed me to turn the oar so it became parallel to the water.

I nodded, gave it a try a few times. It felt clumsy at first, but after a while more natural. Logically it made sense. Leveling the blade during the return would cut down on air drag—again, relating it back to physics. I noticed that the soft pads of my hands were starting to hurt, so I paused and glanced at my fingers.

I blinked, frowned, blinked some more. I had a blister.

Though I had calluses on the tips of my fingers from playing the guitar, there was something really hardcore about having a bleeding blister on one's palm.

"Huh," I said to my hands. I thought it was pretty cool, as it kind of made me feel like a badass.

I'd noticed that all the guys had really rough hands, like *really* rough. Martin's palms and fingers—especially near the joints—were hard. They looked like manly-man hands and I'd made a note of them last semester during one of our lab assignments. I had wondered how this spoiled, entitled rich kid could have such plebeian hands.

He must've noticed my diverted attention because he reached for me, turning my palm toward him for inspection. When he saw the forming blister he frowned severely, lightly touching it with his thumb.

"Damn," he said. I was surprised by how upset he sounded. When he lifted his eyes to mine he looked regretful and troubled.

I gave him a little smile. "I don't mind."

"I do. You should never be hurt."

That statement, and the earnest, stern sincerity with which it was stated, surprised me. Then it laid siege to the remaining defenses around my heart and gently annihilated them. I felt myself melting.

Martin ended up wrapping my hands with medical tape so I wouldn't get any more blisters. Between watching him dreamily, I thought about protesting, but then he made a good point when he said, "That blister is going to tear off and bleed if you don't tape it. If you don't tape them, you won't be able to use them today or tomorrow."

"Why don't you use tape?" I asked as he wound the tape around my fingers.

"I need my hands to be tough. I row almost every day. If you row all the time it's better to let your hands bleed for a while than covering them with tape to protect yourself. If you use tape then you'll have to use it all the time."

"So rather than taking the time to cover your hands, you just toughen up instead? Until you stop bleeding, and you can't get any more blisters because you have so many calluses."

He nodded absentmindedly. "Something like that."

Well...*there* was an apt analogy if I'd ever accidentally stumbled over one. Martin Sandeke was basically his hands. I tucked that thought away for a later discussion.

After hand taping and another half hour of practicing, finally, *finally* they let us row on the open water.

I took Eric's seven-seat, sitting right behind Martin. Eric took three seat so Sam could sit behind him in two-seat. The boat went fast but our movements seemed slow. Martin was careful to set a measured pace, therefore I don't know how fast we were actually traveling. But it felt very fast. It was unsettling at first. I was sure, though I didn't voice it, that I was going to fall into the water. But I didn't.

I didn't even *catch a crab,* which is what it's called when you try to feather your blade too soon or too late and it gets pulled under the water. I was told this usually ends with the oar handle hitting you somewhere on your torso or in your face, or completely throwing you out of the boat (or any combination of the above).

We also turned the boat in a circle using various methods, under Lee's excellent direction.

It was a lot of fun. It was a crazy amount of fun. It was epically fun. When we all moved in unison I felt like I was flying. I loved it. And I could see how rowing might become addictive. There was something about being one with your teammates and the boat, the water and the sky. Something about feeling the rush of the wind, all the while moving your body.

It. Was. Awesome.

But apparently it was also a lot of work because my legs, arms, back, and stomach felt like rubber when we made it back to shore. Sam and I put away the oars as the guys moved the boat. Eric suggested we all go swimming, so we excused ourselves to clean up.

When I finished my shower—my painful, painful shower—I found Sam in her bikini, lying on my bed like she was never going to move from the spot. I put on my swimsuit with a great deal of effort, then collapsed next to her.

"I hurt. I hurt so bad." She said this dramatically, like she might cry. Sam was face down, spread eagle on my mattress. She was clearly exhausted.

"But you had fun." I was also exhausted and lay limply on my side.

Her blue eyes focused on mine, then she gave me a mischievous grin. "It was worth it. I ogled Eric the whole time. I think his back muscles have muscles." Then she added, again sounding in pain, "But I think I'm too sore for sex and that makes me sad."

I laughed, and then winced, my abdominal muscles protesting.

"It's like dating boot camp," she said.

"I think boot camp hurts less."

"That's not what I meant. This, being with Eric all the time, it's like dating boot camp. We've only known each other since Friday but I'm having conversations with him that I never had with any of my previous boyfriends. It's…it's intense."

I nodded—or tried to—thinking about her analogy. "I have no basis for comparison, not really. But you're right. I feel like everything is being rushed, like we're cramming weeks and months of relationship interactions into hours and days."

She gave me a weird, searching look. "Is Martin pushing you?"

"No. But we're…getting close."

"Oh?"

"Yeah."

"And how is that? Are you still convinced he needs just a friend?"

"Yes…and no."

"And…?"

"And what?"

"Don't be coy, I've seen those hickies on your neck. You might be flexible but you didn't give them to yourself."

I narrowed my eyes at her, unwilling to move any other part of my body. "Yes, obviously we're being more than friendly."

"Don't let him pressure you, Kaitlyn."

"It's honestly not like that."

She snorted and rolled her eyes with disbelief. "Yeah, right. I've seen how he looks at you. He wants to have a penis party in your vagina."

I pressed my lips together so I wouldn't laugh, because laughing was painful. "I told him I want to take things slow because, well, I'm the queen of inexperience."

"And he agreed?"

"Yeah. He said he wants us to last, he wants what we do to be meaningful."

"Whoa! He said that?"

"Yes. So we both agreed to slow down, hence the dancing and rowing lessons today."

She smirked, her eyes lighting with mischief. "But he got you off, right?"

Now I rolled my eyes. "Sam…"

"He did. I can tell. You don't need to answer."

"How can you tell?"

"Because you're looking at him like you want him to have a penis party in your vagina."

"Ugh."

"Was it good? Did he use mouth, or hand, or both? I like it when they use both."

"I'm not answering that."

"But it was good, right?"

I blinked at her.

She grinned. "*Niiiice*. Let me know when you're ready to shed your repressed modesty and discuss the baser details. I can tell it was good because of how you're blushing."

"I'm not blushing. It's just warm in here."

"Whatever. I'd high-five you if I could move my arm."

"How do you think I feel? You're already an athlete, I hurt in places I didn't know existed."

"You're the idiot who wanted to learn how to row. Why, Kaitlyn. Why? Why would you do that? Why would you ask that sadist to teach you how to row? Why?"

I tried to shake my head but I couldn't. "I don't know. Shut your whore mouth. I just want to die."

A knock sounded from the door; Sam and I said in unison, "Come in."

Martin poked his head in. I moved only my eyes because even my neck muscles were sore.

"Hey, you ready?"

"No. I've decided to die instead."

He considered me, assessing, then asked, "Are you sore?"

"I would nod but I'm too sore."

Martin strolled into the room, stopping where I lay on the bed, his eyes conducting a slow perusal of my body. "You're going to be sore for a while," he said thoughtfully, his lips twisting to the side. Then he bent down, scooped me up, and brought me to his chest.

"Oh God, I don't even care." I lay limply in his arms, dead weight. "Do whatever you want. I can't even move."

He laughed a little, kissing me lightly then nipping my lower lip. He strode out of the room, calling over his shoulder to Sam, "I'll send Eric in with an anti-inflammatory."

Sam's response was weak and barely audible as he carried me down the hall. "God bless you, Martin Sandeke, even if you are a sadist."

* * *

THE FIRST THING he did was carry me to the lowermost balcony. I didn't even know it existed. It was hidden and down a short path, away from the house. Then he set me gently in a hot tub. The next thing he did was turn and leave.

That's right, he left me. But he was soon forgiven because the hot water felt amazing, my knotted muscles relaxed. Furthermore, he returned with anti-inflammatory medication, a giant glass of water, and a plate of assorted yummy food.

He slipped into the hot tub next to me, seemed to hesitate, and then pulled me between his legs.

I said nothing. I didn't get a chance to say anything because Martin was using his callused hands to massage my back, neck, and shoulders.

I sighed and just gave into it even though it was a definite grey area for No-Touch Tuesday. He might have meant it to be a helpful respite for my sore muscles, but it was making me feel really good in other places.

Like, as you may have guessed, in my pants.

Therefore I groaned. With pleasure. It was a definite pleasure groan. I didn't mean to groan, but it happened, so there it is. I'm a groaner.

His hands stilled; his thumbs were pressing expertly into my lower back and his fingers were wrapped around my waist, massaging my bare stomach. I felt his quads flex at my hips.

"I can't do this if you're going to make those sounds."

"Please, don't stop." I exhaled. It felt so good. I didn't want him to stop. Maybe never.

It was his turn to groan. His forehead met my shoulder. "And you can't say that kind of stuff."

I wiggled, pressing my bottom and spine backward, trying to get him to move his hands again.

"Kaitlyn, you can't move like that either."

"You have a lot of rules," I complained, lifting my hands and placing them on his thighs, trying to get better leverage to push myself into his skilled fingers.

He lifted his forehead from my shoulder, his hands sliding from their relatively benign positions on my body to much less benign positions—like slipping into the cup of my swimsuit top and my pants. I gasped.

When he spoke next his whisper was more growl than whisper. "I know you don't want to be desirable to a man, but it's too fucking late. So stop making me crazy. If you don't want me to touch you, you need to stop teasing me."

Instinctively, I leaned back, my shoulder blades connecting with his chest and my arms coming up out of the water and reaching for his neck.

"I swear, I'm not trying to tease you, and I never said I don't want to be—"

"I heard you earlier, in my room. I heard what you said. It doesn't matter, because I meant it when I said that all I can think about is you." He bit my ear, like he couldn't be close without tasting me, and added, "Honestly, you should be a little scared. I want you in so many ways, and I can't stop thinking about it."

I swallowed past the rising, choking lust that filled my lungs and sent liquid, aching heat to my center. My breathing was shallow, and as such my words were hushed and labored. "Martin, you don't even know me. We've been here for three and a half days. Three and a half days isn't a lot of time."

He released a humorless laugh and it sent an odd chill down my spine. Slowly, very slowly, almost like it was meant to be more of a caress than a withdrawal, he removed his hands from the sweet spots where he touched me and his fingers closed over my upper arms. He lifted me up just slightly so he could move to the other side of the hot tub, placing as much distance between us as was possible in the small space.

He swallowed, focusing on some spot over my head for a long time, gathering himself—his thoughts, his self-control—before bringing the full weight of his gaze back to mine, pinning me in place.

When he spoke, his voice was hypnotic, soothing, and darkly unapologetic. "Parker, you've been the star of all my wet dreams since the first day of lab in the fall. I'm beyond caring whether you know... I've been watching you. I know you drink your coffee black and always from the same Doctor Who mug. Your favorite band is Weezer, or you just have an incredible amount of Weezer concert T-shirts. I know you mumble synonyms to yourself and it's fucking adorable. I know you look for ways to help people, like giving that girl in lab a safety pin when her shirt ripped, or offering your notes to that douchebag, Kenneth."

"You remember that?" My eyes moved between his, fascinated, enthralled, shocked.

"Yes, and all the other quiet acts of kindness over the last six months. As well as the fact that you're the only girl who has ever refused to give me her phone number."

I was struck by an unhappy thought. "Is this...am I just some kind of challenge for you?"

He shook his head, looking disappointed in me for asking the question. "No. You are not a challenge to me or a problem to be solved. I want to be *with* you, all the time. Did you think it was just a coincidence we were paired as partners two semesters in a row?"

My mouth fell open and I'm sure my eyebrows were doing strange things on my forehead. A little squeak of disbelief escaped my lips, but overall I was speechless. This was...this was...I was...

Shocked, stunned, surprised, bewildered, confused, bemused, befuddled.

I would have been distressed, except for the fact that Martin had been starring in all my dirty fantasies since the first day of lab in the fall.

I cleared my throat as I thought this over, considering how best to respond. When I was on the precipice of taking too long, I blurted, "I have to be honest, Martin. If you weren't so hot, this would be really distressing. But, for some reason, the fact that you're hot negates the creepiness factor."

His mouth tugged to the side, though his eyes and voice were hard. "Lucky me."

"And also in the spirit of honesty, I've been thinking about you too, mostly your body and face and eyes…but I didn't like you very much before this trip."

"I know. I was always trying to think of ways to get you to see me, talk to me, but you were always looking the other way."

"But I *did* see you. I saw when you fought that guy in the dining hall last semester, and I saw you yell at that girl outside the Basic Sciences building in October and make her cry."

Martin stared at me, some of the glacial frigidity thawing as he considered me. Then he said, "No wonder you thought I was an asshole."

Before I could think better of it, I shrugged and said, "You kind of are an asshole."

He exhaled a surprised laugh, but amazed me by saying, "Yeah. I guess I am. But I don't like to be used, Parker. Do you know how often people ask me for money? People who I considered friends? Do you know how many girls want to throw themselves on my dick? It's not about me. It's about greed. I'm not bored of it. I *hate* it. I've had a life-time of people trying to leverage me to get what they want. And if I'm an asshole it might have something to do with that."

I nodded, remembering the conversation I'd overheard just a few days ago in the lab cabinet, the catalyst for all of this. That girl was going to drug him, assault him, rape him, and hope to get *pregnant*— all for money. She didn't want him. She obviously didn't even know him.

I added absentmindedly, "Kind of like the calluses on your hands."
"What?"

I stared at him for a beat, wondering if he'd appreciate or be irri-tated by the analogy. I decided this was No-Touch Tuesday, and tomorrow was Wet-and-Wild Wednesday. If I was going to decide whether or not to participate, then I needed to be as honest and forth-right as possible now.

"The calluses on your hands. They're purposeful, meant to protect you in the long run. They're armor, so that you can't be hurt. Just like how you treat people…callously."

His eyes narrowed on me, grew meditative, introspective, but not hostile. He said nothing.

I continued, "You're callous because you have to be. Because otherwise you'd be bleeding all the time."

Martin's face did a funny thing then; he looked like a wounded animal. His eyes flashed, grew at once guarded and distant. His sudden reaction and the gathering ferocity in his stare set my heart hammering. I'd obvi-ously touched on a nerve, because he now looked slightly dangerous.

I tried to think of something to say that could diffuse this change in his demeanor, but before I could, he asked, "What about you?" The tone of his voice told me he was very close to losing his temper.

"Me?"

"Yeah, you."

"Uh, what about me?"

"What about your calluses?"

I turned my face to the side, administering him a sideways look. "My calluses?"

"Yes. You're not exactly a very feeling person." He said these words quite callously, the wall between us now feeling like an actual, tangible thing.

"I'm not…? What?" The hairs on the back of my neck rose, but I didn't know if it was because his question was confusing or because my subconscious was warning me that I was venturing near a trap. "I'm a feeling person. I care about people."

"I'm not talking about empathy for other people. I'm talking about *you*…feeling." His eyes darted over me and when he spoke next it was as though he were speaking to himself. "You're controlled, childish, and repressed."

My mouth dropped open; I pointed to myself with my thumbs and my voice was dripping with incredulity. "Repressed? Childish?"

"Sponge Bob Square Pants pajamas?"

"So? What's wrong with Sponge Bob? He's funny."

"Don't you want to feel sexual?"

Now my scalp was itching, my throat was tight, and I could hear the blood rushing between my ears. I had to take a calming breath before I could speak because I was angry, and I didn't know why I was angry.

"Of course."

He shook his head slowly, surveying me. "I don't think so."

"Why? Because I wasn't ready for you to...to...put your mouth on my private area?"

"See. You can't even say it."

"I can say it." I crossed my arms over my chest, the hot tub suddenly felt too hot.

"Then say it, Kaitlyn." He grinned, and it looked wolfish. "Say the words. Say *fuck me with your tongue.*"

I gathered a deep breath, glared at him and his predatory smile, and prepared myself to say the words. Then I held my breath. Then I gritted my teeth. Then I narrowed my eyes.

"You can't say it," he whispered, looking triumphant and sad—not for himself, but for me. I comprehended that he felt sorry for me.

I released the breath and looked away, my blush now crimson. My anger was multiplied by mortification, my stomach a storm of dismay and disappointment. Why couldn't I say it? What the hell was wrong with me? I squeezed my eyes shut then covered my face with my hands. I felt like crying, it was so ridiculous.

Seconds passed in relative silence while I tried to get myself under control. But it wasn't working. I was going to cry.

Abruptly Martin said, "I wish you wouldn't do that."

"Do what?" I snapped.

"You always cover your face when we talk."

I sensed rather than heard him draw closer. When he put his hands on my wrists, I jumped, startled even though I knew he'd crossed the barrier between us.

"Let me see you." His grip tightened—firm but not hurtful—and pulled my hands away.

I was crying. Not big messy sobs, because that's not how I cried. When I cried it was silent and usually into my pillow. And I didn't cry often. The last time I'd cried was when my cat died in my junior year of high school. My mother had added an item to our weekly agenda: *New cat for Kaitlyn - Pros/Cons.*

"Why are you like this?" Martin's voice startled me because it was so...gentle.

I lifted my watery eyes to his and had to bite my bottom lip to keep my chin from wobbling; his gaze matched his gentle tone. He looked a little concerned and a lot curious.

"What's so scary about being seen?"

I cleared my throat and glanced over his shoulder. "Just because I'm not ready to take the next step in the physical intimacy pyramid doesn't mean I'm afraid to be seen."

"I agree, it doesn't. But you *are* terrified, Kaitlyn. Everything is logical discussions with you, everything is so reasonable and analytical. Don't you feel passionate about anything?"

"Of course."

"What?"

"...I love my parents." I said this lamely, because it was lame. Not that loving one's parents is lame, but rather the only thing I could come up with that at all resembled passion was loving my parents.

"That's not what I'm talking about and you know it."

I slid my teeth to the side, not sure what to say.

Martin turned, bringing me with him, and settled into a seat. He pulled me, his hands moving on my body to position me as he liked, until I was facing him, my legs straddling his hips. And I let him because I felt lost. This conversation was confusing.

Passion...was a confusing concept to me, which was—in and of itself—a weird thing to be confused about. I chided myself, feeling abruptly clumsy and stupid, and yes, childish. How could passion be so foreign? I'd read enough books about it. I knew, theoretically, what it involved. I felt a degree of passion for books and geek culture, short-bread cookies, and my favorite bands. As well, I'd felt something close to passionate about music once upon a time.

My mother and I had talked through why this passion for music was both good and bad.

It was good to have an appreciation for the arts. As a whole, the arts enriched society.

But it was bad to be passionate, focus energy on something, when I had talents in other areas of greater need, talents that were scarcer and in greater need by society.

She explained that the world didn't need more musicians. But it did need more female—especially female—scientists, mathe-maticians, politicians, physicians, and leaders. I was good at my music, but being just good would likely never yield the results necessary to support myself as a musician. Nor would I have a directly positive and lasting benefit to society as just a good musi-cian. It was much better to focus on math and science, areas where I was already gifted, areas where I could make a tangible difference.

I was lost in these thoughts, my tears having ebbed, when I became aware that Martin was staring at me, watching me. I felt his gaze scan my form. He'd paused, as though considering me, then brushed his knuckles over the swell of my breast.

My breath hitched and my gaze jumped to his.

"There," he said, his eyes searching mine as he touched me again, this time also tugging the strap of my top down and baring my breast. His other hand trailed along the column of my throat to my shoulder then collarbone, tickling me. I shivered and sighed. "There it is. You have it, and when I touch you like this, it's there."

I could only look at him in response. I didn't want to move even though we were breaking the No-Touch Tuesday rule. I was caught in rule-versus-want purgatory. Ultimately, I decided not to move, and No-Touch Tuesday could go help itself to jumping off a cliff.

His hands slid down my sides, stomach, and hips. Under the water, he used the backs of his fingers on the inside of my thighs and I tensed, paying no heed to my sore muscles.

"I understand that you're not ready for me to fuck your sweet pussy with my tongue. I do. I understand." His whispered words sent a lightning strike of white-hot longing through me. I felt like I might break in half.

He continued, all the while his fingers stroked back and forth, each time coming closer to my center. "If you help me soften my calluses, I'll help you soften yours."

I swallowed, feeling dazed. "How?"

"Be passionate."

I shook my head, a dizzy denial spilling from my lips. "I'm just not built that way."

"From where I'm sitting, you are." Martin growled this then leaned forward to steal a quick kiss, his mouth leaving a trail from my jaw to my neck, whispering after biting my ear, "You are. You've just... turned it off, buried it for some reason."

"Why do you even care?"

"Because, Kaitlyn, and I don't know how many times you're going to make me say this, I care about you, I want *you*."

"But why—"

"Why do people care about each other? What is attraction? I can't give you a list of reasons why I react to you like I do. This isn't an equation to balance. You're the one I'm always thinking about. It's you. It just is."

"You need to rethink that list, because what if I'm just...asexual?" I felt unsteady and sensitized; the hot, balmy, bubbly water licking my bare breasts and back. As such my words were breathless, labored.

He leaned back, captured and held my gaze before speaking. "This isn't about sex, Parker. But for the record, you're sexy as fuck. I'm talking about passion. Wanting something. Loving it. I'm passionate about rowing, and I'm passionate about knowing how everything works and telling other people what to do." He smirked at this last thought, then his eyes grew staid and thoughtful. Martin's knuckles skimmed up my inner thigh and finally, *finally* touched my center. He rubbed the back of his middle finger up and down the apex between my spread legs, whispering, "And I'm passionate about you."

My breath hitched, needy and painful spikes of pleasure originating from where he touched me, singing through my body. These sensations were unwieldy, unmanageable, and I realized it was because I believed him. I believed he was passionate about me.

"Touching you right now is meaningful for me. Tasting you, taking you now, here, would be meaningful for me." He removed his fingers and my thighs tightened. Ignoring my reflexive protest, he lifted his hands out of the water, and then pulled my bikini straps back up my shoulders. He covered me as he said, "But it's not going to be meaningful for you...unless you're passionate about me."

[4]
THE DISCOVERY OF ATOMIC STRUCTURE

I T WAS PAST midnight and I was lying in the middle of my giant bed, staring out the skylight to the stars above.

Neither Martin nor I spoke much after we left the hot tub. I couldn't. I guessed he sensed that I couldn't, so he let me be.

Sam was not currently with me in my super-huge king-sized bed tonight. I saw her briefly at dinner, but then she and Eric and a few of the other guys decided to go for a moonlight swim. I'd been mostly quiet during the meal and didn't want to go to the beach. I felt...morose.

Therefore I excused myself, ignoring Martin's watchful glare as I left, and hid away in my gigantic suite.

Martin was right. I was analytical—overly so—and I'd been using it as a way to suppress passion. Everything could be reasoned away or made to look silly with enough rational scrutiny. Faith, love, hope, lust, anger, sadness, compassion—everything.

And that's what I'd been doing with every feeling and emotion that was confusing or difficult to control. Except, when Martin touched me I felt a little out of control...or rather, a lot out of control. I felt unsteady, I felt uncertain, I felt...

I *felt*.

I rolled to my left side; instead of staring out the skylight, I stared at the wall of windows overlooking the beach.

Passion and being passionate were not bad things. Just like arsenic isn't bad, even though it can be used to murder a person. If passion wasn't bad, then why was the very idea of *being passionate* so terrifying?

I sighed, rearranged myself in the bed—again—and punched my pillow. My pillow was seriously getting on my nerves. It wasn't reading my mind and supporting my neck like I needed. I considered breaking up with my pillow, but then decided to give it one more chance. Settling back on the mattress, this time on my right side, I squeezed my eyes shut and willed myself to go to sleep.

I couldn't.

My body was sore, yes. But it wasn't why I couldn't sleep. I felt restless, I felt irritated, I felt dissatisfied, I felt…

I *felt*.

Abruptly I sat up in bed and threw the pillow across the room. I *felt* like it was giving me inadequate neck support and I hated it. I hated that pillow with passion.

We were never ever, ever, ever getting back together.

I tossed the covers to one side and bolted out of the gargantuan suite. Its largeness was overwhelming and I needed small. I needed safe. I wandered around the house for a bit, intent at first on a visit to the kitchen because...cookies. But at the last minute I took a right instead of a left, went up the stairs instead of down, and found myself in the room with the piano and the guitars.

I hovered at the door and stared at the piano. It was a Steinway grand and it was gorgeous - black and sleek and curvy. Moonlight spilling in through the windows gave it a shadowy, secretive appearance. I wanted to touch it. For some reason, in that moment, it felt forbidden.

It made no sense.

You're being silly, as it's just a piano, I thought. But then I pushed that thought away because it felt too rational. Instead I embraced the sensation of *feeling*. This act, coming here in the middle of the night to touch and play the piano, excited me because it felt forbidden. So I let it be something dangerous, even if in reality it wasn't, because it made my heart beat faster and my breath quicken.

I closed the door behind me and tiptoed to the instrument. I sat on the bench, wincing when it creaked just slightly under my weight. I set my fingers on the ivory keys and closed my eyes. Inexplicably—irrationally—they felt warm to the touch, soft and smooth.

Then I played the piano.

At first I played a few songs from memory—Chopin, Beethoven, Strauss—then I bluffed my way through a jazzy version of *Piano Man*, by Billy Joel. Then I bluffed my way through something new, slow and morose, a composition of my own making that had no beginning and no end. It was nonsense because it was the middle, and everyone knows songs have to have a beginning and end.

My lack of adhering to common sense and established norms also felt forbidden and dangerous. It was dangerous because it was altering. Altering me. I felt myself change, shift in some fundamental way as I played entirely in the bass clef.

It was my song.

So what if it never started or ended?

So what if it was nonsense?

So what?

It was mine and its lack of rationality was seductive. I loved it. It was beautiful to me.

"Prudence," I said to the empty room, my left hand moving unhurriedly over the keys. "Practicality, good judgment, reasonableness, rationality, realism…" Each word was punctuated with a chord in the key of B minor.

Schubert was said to regard B minor as a key expressing a quiet acceptance of fate, but I was using it now as a battle cry. My right hand joined my left to marry treble and bass, the sweet descant like cries and sighs of melancholy.

But then I realized the cries weren't coming from the piano. They were coming from me. I was crying. I *for real* cried, loud and messy and angry. I gave myself over to it, and the piece became *incalzando*—

louder, faster—and it felt good to lose control. Like a release. Like unearthing something essential, but up to this point buried.

I didn't angry-cry for very long; my tears reached their crescendo and so did the song…and then I just couldn't play anymore. I stopped mid stanza, folded my arms on the music rest, then buried my head and cried.

They weren't my normal sedate tears, however. They were still messy and raw. Uncontrolled and unsteady. Restless and irritated. Dissatisfied. They were tears of passion.

Someplace, closer to the surface than I would like, a version of Kaitlyn Parker was rolling her eyes at my dramatics, wanting to point out all the ways I was being epicurean and childish.

I was able to keep her at bay because I wasn't being childish. In fact, I was finally *not* being childish. I was waking up from a deep slumber, where the only two things that mattered were being smart and being safe. I was taking the first step toward leaving that behind for something infinitely frightening, for a kaleidoscope of feelings.

The hand on my shoulder made me jump and scared the bejebus out of me. I sucked in a shocked breath, but then immediately released it in a whoosh of relief when I found Martin was the owner of the hand. He was idling behind me.

I huffed another breath, my heart still beating staccato as I calmed myself. I glanced up at him and pointed out the obvious, "You scared me."

He didn't respond. I couldn't see his face very well, but from what I could discern he appeared to be staring at me with something like violent absorption. It was…unnerving. I wiped tears from my cheeks and laughed a little, giving an inch into the instinct to feel silly.

"I don't even know what I'm doing here," I said, shaking my head.

"Parker, you said you could play the piano."

I nodded. "Yeah. I mean, yes. I dabble mostly."

"Dabble?"

I pressed my lips together, liquid feelings still leaking out of my eyes. "Yes. Dabble."

"That's not dabbling. That's mastery."

I flinched at his compliment, then immediately shrugged it off. I began to rise, turn away from him. He caught me by the shoulders and turned me to face him, my bottom hitting the piano keys and making a clumsy chord.

"You are an *artist*." He shook me a little as he said this, his eyes darting between mine like this—what he was saying—was of vital importance. "Why aren't you a music major?"

I automatically scoffed and he pushed the bench to the side with a swift nudge from his knee, then stepped into my space, annihilating the distance between us. The hollow, awkward notes from where my backside still pressed against the keys created an eerie, off-tune soundtrack to what was quickly feeling like another confrontation.

"I'm pretty good, but I'm not amazing."

His gaze searched mine again and his features twisted until they communicated that he thought I was crazy.

"Why are you lying to yourself? What kind of bullshit is this? What I just heard, that wasn't *pretty good*. That was…that was spectacular. That was once in a lifetime."

My chin wobbled, and Martin was growing blurry as new tears filled my eyes. I shook my head in denial but I couldn't speak. I felt too raw. I felt too vulnerable.

I *felt*.

Martin's eyes were devouring my face, like he was seeing me for the first time, or he was seeing a new me, and he was afraid that this vision was fleeting.

"You," he breathed on a harsh sigh, like the word was torn from deep inside him. I watched him swallow and he appeared to be struggling, fighting against some invisible monster or tide, rising above him and preparing to wash his world away.

He said nothing else, though he looked like he wanted to. Instead he caught my cheek in his palm, and pressed an ardent kiss to my lips. His other hand settled firmly on the base of my spine and brought me against him.

My movement was restricted because he held me so completely; therefore I slid my hands under the hem of his shirt and gripped his rigid sides, loving his smooth, taut skin. I rubbed myself against him, sought to deepen the kiss, a little wild with the irrationality of just feeling.

But then he pulled away, turned away, and crossed to the far side of the room. I slouched, trying to catch my breath, and I heard him curse viciously. Yet almost immediately he turned back and charged at me, muttering another curse before he pressed me more completely against the piano, insinuating himself between my legs.

Again, the discordant music caused by my bottom and thighs was nonsensical and jarring. Nonetheless, my heart swelled at the harsh melody, because it *felt* real and honest. Martin rocked into me and I sucked in a surprised breath. His erection was unyielding—granite, hard and covetous—and he rubbed himself against my center with an impatience that felt forbidden, dangerous, and seductive.

As well his hands were everywhere, searching, grabbing, wanting, and grasping as though he would remain forever disgruntled with settling for just one place, one touch. They slid under my shirt, pushing it up, insisting I discard the offensive garment. I lifted my arms to assist and he whipped it off, his mouth tasting and biting my collarbone.

His hands cupping my bottom, Martin lifted me off my feet and turned, supporting my weight entirely. He brought me to the side of the instrument. Abruptly he lifted me higher, then relinquished my weight to the piano. He buried his face in my breasts while he showered them with all good things—some painful, some tender, all wonderful—then pushed me gently backward until my back met with the cool lacquer of the instrument. My legs dangled off the side.

"Martin, what—"

"Let me," he said, his thumbs rubbing a controlled circle around the tight peaks at the center of my breasts, then sliding his hands down my stomach, to the waist of my plain, grey sleep shorts. He curled his fingers around the band, then moved to my bottom, lifting my hips. He tugged the band lower, pulling my shorts and underwear over my hips, bottom, and thighs.

I stared at him as he did this and his gaze didn't deviate from mine.

When my pajamas hit the floor his hands slid up my calves, the backs of my knees, the underside of my thighs, lifting my legs as he went until he'd positioned my heels on the edge of the piano, my legs immodestly spread.

Then his gaze flickered away and he looked at me. I held my breath. Waiting. Watching.

Martin licked his lips, his thumbs at my center opening me. Then he bent and placed a cherishing, closed-mouth kiss directly on my clitoris, his soft, full lips lingering at my apex.

"Oh God."

I panted. I tensed. My hands gripping the smooth surface of the piano and finding no purchase. Every part of me sore and throbbing from my earlier exercise, yet singularly focused on where his lips loved my body. He leaned away slightly and kissed the inside of my thigh, nipped at the skin, then soothed it with his tongue, trailing a wet path directly to my slick center. He licked me, softly, reverently. Then he licked me again, and again.

He tasted me over and over; wet, lapping noises that struck me as tremendously carnal married with my harsh breaths and moans. The combination was discordant, awkward, and clumsy; yet like the accidental and inharmonious tones of the piano as he'd pressed me against the keys, the sounds were real and they were honest.

They were the sounds of sex, of desire.

If I hadn't been lost to my passion, if I'd heard the sounds separate from this act, they might have struck me as lascivious and animalistic, repugnant. But passion changed them. Passion changed us. Passion changed *me*.

His fingers whispered over the backs of my thighs, making my legs shake. I threaded my fingers through his hair, pressing him to me, needing to hold onto him. Then he did something shocking and wonderful. Keeping his lips on my center, his tongue lapping me loudly, hungrily, he moved his index and middle finger into my body and stroked.

My breath hitched, my hips lifted off the piano, and I felt my insides shatter into a million shards of pleasure. It felt so good it hurt—

the sharp edges of my release cutting through me, leaving a trail of ruin and stunning anguish. My lungs seized as I tried to hold on to the sensation, willing it to last and last.

But it didn't. It couldn't. And when the shards dissolved and disappeared, leaving me cut and wounded and satiated and defenseless, I realized I was crying again.

Not big messy sobs.

Just quiet, joyful tears.

I didn't think about them, whether they made sense or what Martin might think. I didn't try to reason them away or analyze the pros and cons of tears after cunnilingus.

I felt cherished.

I *felt*.

And it felt like perfection.

* * *

I SLEPT NAKED in Martin's bed. Yep. True Story.

Well, Martin slept. I didn't sleep much. I couldn't.

After our early morning inauguration to Wet-and-Wild Wednesday, Martin wrapped me in a blanket and carried me to his room, leaving my clothes strewn all around the piano. I was deposited on his twin bed. He then pulled off his shirt—but left on his pajama pants—and climbed under the covers next to me. He wrapped an arm around my torso and pulled my bare back to his bare front, slipped his leg between mine, and cupped my breast with his palm.

Then I felt him sigh. It sounded content and it made me smile. I had to bite my bottom lip to keep from laughing because the noise made me so happy.

"What?" His voice penetrated the darkness, sounding curious and maybe a little concerned. "What's wrong?"

I shook my head, willing myself not to laugh.

"Tell me."

I mimicked his sigh, but said nothing.

He stilled, waited, his hand at my breast toying with it, with me. I tried to ignore the lovely stabs of pleasure caused by his ministrations, coiling again in my lower belly.

Out of the blue he blurted, "We should move in together."

My eyes flew open. All thought was bulldozed straight out of my brain by Martin's statement.

"I…what?"

Martin pinched my nipple, rolling it between his thumb and fore-finger, causing me to hiss and tense, then he smoothed his hand from my shoulder, down my ribs, over my side, over my hip, until it cupped my bottom. He caressed me there, like touching my body was his favorite thing to do.

This time when I sighed it wasn't meant to mimic. It was a sigh of pure contentment. Who knew that lying in Martin's bed, having one's bottom stroked could feel so good?

"I said," he whispered against my ear, "we should move in together. When we get back we'll start looking for places."

"That seems terribly impetuous and likely to end badly." My voice was lazy, soft, and not at all argumentative.

"It won't end at all, Kaitlyn." He kissed my shoulder, then smacked my backside once. "Now I need to get some sleep or else I'm going to be dead for practice tomorrow."

And with that he resumed our position—bringing me against him, hand at my breast—and fell quickly asleep.

Meanwhile, I did not.

It was one thing to be passionate, it was quite another to let passion be the sole driving force in my life. Reason and rationality still had a place at the table, even if passion wanted to have sex on aforementioned table.

So I spent at least another hour and a half reasoning my way through this latest and unexpected minefield. Because I wasn't going to move in with Martin unless I trusted him completely, unless ground rules were established, discussed and negotiated, unless we were both on the same page. *Unless I was in love with him.*

And I didn't and we hadn't and we weren't. And I wasn't…at least, not yet.

[5]

SIMPLE ORGANIC COMPOUNDS

I KNOW I fell asleep because I was eventually woken up, and the waker-upper was a demon sent from hell.

"What the actual fuck is going on in here?"

This question was shrieked very loudly, and startled me into a sitting position on Martin's bed. Instinctively, I grabbed the sheet to cover myself. I blinked through my sleep and glanced frantically around the room, worried it was on fire or about to explode—because why else would someone be yelling at me?

I brought the shrieker into focus and frowned at her. I had no idea who she was. I wondered for about two seconds if I was still dreaming and in my dream I was being harangued by an insane wet T-shirt contestant, or a woman made homeless by her penchant for elective plastic surgery.

"Pardon me...I'm...what?" I asked her sleepily, figuring if she were merely a figment of my imagination she would disappear.

She didn't disappear.

"I said," she ground out between clenched teeth, her hands coming to her slim, Barbie-doll like hips, "what the actual fuck is going on in here? Who the actual fuck are you?"

I blinked at her, knowing definitely this was not a dream. I would never dream a person who used the phrase "the actual fuck" unless that person was a parrot trapped in a human's body and didn't know any better.

"I was sleeping," I answered honestly, pushing my hair out of my face. I shook my head to clear the cobwebs as I looked around. I was in Martin's room and the events of the prior night abruptly rushed back. I didn't have any time to organize my thoughts because the woman was still glaring at me, so I continued, stating the obvious. "But now you're yelling at me and I don't know who you are."

Her head did this strange bobbing/pivot thing on her neck, which really made her look like a parrot. This of course surprised me, though I successfully fought the sudden urge to burst out laughing.

"*You* don't know who *I* am? What the actual fuck?!" she shrieked.

I took a deep breath and leaned back against the headboard of the bed. I clutched the sheet to my chest as I surveyed her, noting this was definitely one of those occasions where passion served no purpose.

She was tiny, maybe five one, and very tanned. She was also wearing platform sandals that added four or five inches to her height. She also had very small hips and very thin legs. But her boobs were as big as mine, maybe a little bigger, and truly gave her the unnatural proportional appearance of a Barbie doll. Her eyes were pale blue, her hair was bleach—and I mean *bleach*—blonde; it fell like straw around her shoulders and likely reached her tiny bottom.

She was wearing blue eyeshadow and pink lipstick and there was just something really wrong about her lips and lack of facial expression. Though she was shrieking her face never seemed to alter its expression. It was eerie.

"I'll tell you who I am, and then you're going to get the actual fuck out of Martin's room, leave this house, and never talk to him again." She sounded angry. Her words told me she was angry, but her dead-face was distracting and fascinating.

She pointed to her sternum, the place between her giant, balloon-shaped boobs. "*I* am Mrs. Sandeke, Mart-*tin*'s stepmother…? You see? I own this house and you need to leave."

I didn't like how she said his name. It was…possessive, and…creepy.

"Oh," I said, nodding. "Nice to meet you." I cringed after the automatic words left my mouth, because they would likely sound insincere given the situation; therefore, now flustered, I rushed through the rest of my thought. "Um, well, if you'll give me a few minutes to get my things then I'll be out of your—"

"No." Martin's voice thundered from someplace down the hall and pulled Mrs. Sandeke's attention over her shoulder.

He wasn't running when he entered his room—seemingly careful not to touch her as he slipped past where she hovered at the door—but he sure was walking fast. His eyes held mine as he approached the bed, then he bent down, cupped the back of my head, and gave me a quick, soft kiss.

"Hey, you okay?" Martin looked genuinely concerned, maybe a little panicked, and his eyes darted between mine. I barely had time to nod before he said, "I'll take care of this, don't worry about a thing. You're staying with me."

"Mart-*tin*! What the actual fuck?" This time she didn't shriek. She whined.

Martin's eyes rolled back and I saw he gritted his teeth as he straightened and stood, turned and faced his stepmother.

"Can you get her to stop saying that? It's really irritating," I muttered to his back, hopefully low enough that only Martin would hear.

"Patrice," he said, crossing his arms over his chest, "you need to get out of my room."

Everything became very, very still.

Leave it to Martin to intone so much with slowly and softly spoken words. They dripped with icicles, icicles of hate. I actually felt the temperature of the room drop at least five degrees. I hoped he never spoke to me like that.

"But…but Mar-*tin*…" Her voice became very baby-like, high pitched. It was weird.

I couldn't see her because Martin was blocking my view, but I imagined her expression didn't alter because...dead-face.

"You know you are *never* allowed in any of my rooms."

"But," she sighed softly, like a bird cooing, "you know you don't mean that."

"You disgust me. You're repulsive. You married my father for his money and have been trying to fuck me ever since. Climbing in bed with a fourteen-year-old boy is not okay, Patrice."

I flinched, and my mouth fell open in shock, my eyes expanding to their maximum aperture. There was family dysfunction, and then there was Martin's family. This was crazy. This was Jerry Springer meets Lifestyles of the Rich and Famous meets The Count of Monte Cristo.

"Why...what...why..." Patrice huffed and puffed, sounding lost and alarmed. "I don't know what you're talking about."

"I want Kaitlyn to know. I want her to know what being with me means, what disgusting baggage I carry in the form of family members."

The room fell silent, and I felt another shift in the temperature of the room; it grew even colder.

"Fine," Patrice said, her voice now alto, sounding *entirely* different...like a completely different person.

Instinctively I leaned to the side to see if a new woman had taken her place. It was still her, but her posturing had changed. Her shoulders were thrown back and her chin was tilted stubbornly upward. Other than that, her face looked the same, because...dead-face.

Patrice crossed her arms over her chest and added, "But you should do this skank someplace else, not in my house."

"This isn't your house. This is my house. All the houses are *my* houses. Everything is in *my* name. Everything was put in my name before my father married you, because he knows you'd divorce him, screw him over in a heartbeat if you thought you could walk away with more than a few hundred thousand dollars."

What the what? His house?

This statement—or reminder, I was guessing—didn't make her

happy. The room temperature dropped again. I wondered if it would snow.

Obviously feeling cornered and nasty, Patrice decided to go for the personal approach. "You like this type of girl? The chubby ones do it for you?"

"Don't." The single word, again softly and slowly spoken, sent chills down my spine. It was more than a warning; it was a threat and it sounded lethal.

She held her hands up. "Whatever. I don't care. But I will enjoy tearing her to pieces and making her life hell and using your money to do it."

He chuckled at this. "That's funny, Patrice."

She cocked her head to the side as he laughed. "What? What's so funny?"

"This girl right here," he motioned to me, sounding proud and coldly amused, "this girl is Kaitlyn *Parker*, as in *Senator* Parker's daughter. You know, potentially the first female president of the United States in the next election cycle? As in the granddaughter of Colonel Timothy Parker, the *astronaut*. She's untouchable. She's a national treasure. You do something to her, the entire fucking world will bring pain to your doorstep."

I'd never thought of myself in these terms, not really. Nothing he said was untrue, but living the reality of being a perceived national treasure and accepting it were two entirely different states. Therefore, hearing this declaration come from Martin's mouth—like *he had* thought about it—made my brain stutter and a spike of alarm shoot up my neck.

Patricia's eyes slid to mine and, miracle of miracles, her expression did change. The color left her face and her eyes seemed to dim. Meanwhile I sat motionless in the bed, not sure what I should be feeling.

Then Martin added, obviously enjoying himself a great deal, "That's right. She's a goddamn national treasure, and she's my girl-friend, *and* you need to get the fuck out of my house before I decide to stop being so nice to you."

[6]
DIMENSIONAL ANALYSIS

U *NBELIEVABLE.*
That's the word that kept flying around my stunned brain. I couldn't even play the synonym game with the word. It was just all completely, totally, entirely, wholly, and absolutely unbelievable.

It was, the entire exchange was, epically unbelievable.

Patricia Sandeke—fourth, latest, and longest-lasting wife of Martin's father—was…truly a different species. I know it's not PC to think ill of my fellow females. In fact, one of my life rules is to try to assume the best of people, but—I'm sorry and I'm not sorry—the woman was a miserable excuse for a human being. She was a carica-ture, the epitome of a scheming, blonde bimbo gold digger.

Maybe she had hidden layers and a secret pain that explained away all her terrible behavior.

Maybe I was being a petulant and judgmental harpy.

Or maybe there were no hidden layers or depth. Maybe there weren't two sides to this story. Maybe she was a black hole of vapidity and greed.

And Martin…

I tried to swallow. My mouth was dry, and therefore my throat was parched. I hazarded a glance at him but then quickly looked away before he saw my sneak peek.

I didn't honestly know what to think about Martin.

At present he was staring straight again, the set of his jaw grim, the clouds in his blue eyes menacing. We were speeding away from the house via a fancy speedboat.

I didn't know anything about boats, but I knew this one was super fancy for a speedboat. It was like a mini yacht. We were in an enclosed cabin aboveboard that looked over the bow; Martin was sitting in the elevated captain's chair and I was in the co-pilot seat to his left. Both chairs reminded me of splendidly plush, leather barstools with armrests.

The vessel even had a downstairs bedroom with portal windows for undersea viewing. The space was much larger than I'd expected from first glance of the boat hull; it had room enough for a double bed, dresser, desk, bathroom, efficiency kitchen, two closets, and a respectably sized sitting area.

He hadn't said more than two words since we left the house. But before we left, in his room, he explained that he'd cut morning practice short when Mrs. Greenstone radioed Lee in the boat about Martin's father and stepmother's unexpected arrival.

After the showdown at the *I'm not OK Corral*, otherwise known as Martin's bedroom, he gave me one of his shirts and a pair of his shorts so I could get dressed. Then he left and told me to lock the door after him.

To me it all felt clandestine, cloak and dagger, high dramatics.

To Martin however, I suspected it felt like a Wednesday.

He returned ten minutes later with my things and informed me I would be sleeping with him for the duration of my stay. I opened my mouth to question this, but then he added that the gargantuan suite was the master suite, and Mr. Sandeke had claimed it for himself.

I wanted to point out that there were other rooms in the house, but Martin's severe and distracted scowl made me back off. I decided to just go with it...for now.

I changed into my own clothes before we left, but I made him turn around while I dressed. Being naked at night with a happy Martin felt different than being naked during the day with an angry Martin. Yes, the odd modesty rules were likely my own dysfunctions rearing their ugly heads, but I didn't have time for self-psychoanalysis. Martin wanted us to leave the house, and do so as quickly as possible.

He busied himself by stuffing some of my things and his things into an overnight bag.

When I was finished changing, I risked his ire by asking, "What about Sam? We can't leave her here."

"Eric has Sam. He's taking her to the cottage on the other side of the island. We're going to meet them there tomorrow. Everyone else, all the other guys, are flying back today." He didn't look at me as he said this, as he was too focused on his task of merging the essentials of our belongings into one small bag.

"Tomorrow? She's staying?"

"Yeah, I figured you wouldn't stay without her, so..." He sighed, picking up my chemistry book. After considering the cover for three seconds, he put it in the bag.

I guessed he didn't want to chance another encounter with his wicked stepmother. Or maybe it was his father he dreaded seeing. Or maybe both.

Sitting next to him now, while he steered his fancy speedboat with livid concentration, I didn't know what to say.

When I thought about relationships, I had thought the role of the significant other was to know what to say. My parents always seemed to know what to say to each other. But then, my parents had been married for thirty years and hadn't been raised by evil people.

I'd only been conversing (about topics other than chemistry) with Martin for six days. Granted, those six days had included quite a lot of conversing. Sam had been right when she'd said this week was rela-tionship boot camp. I was certainly getting bang for my time buck.

But the fact remained I didn't know Martin well enough to know what to say, or if I should say anything at all. So I fretted instead until he slowed the boat to an idle, stopped it, then cut the engine.

I glanced around us. We were some distance away from the southernmost tip of the island and no other boats were nearby. We were completely alone.

"This was a mistake."

Martin's distracted statement drew my attention. I studied him for a beat, wondering if he were planning to continue unprompted.

When he remained silent, his eyes examining the gauges on the dashboard in front of him, I decided to ask, "What was a mistake?"

"Bringing you here, to the island. We should have just stayed on campus; my father wouldn't have bothered us there. But I thought..." Martin absentmindedly covered his mouth with one hand, lifted his eyes to the horizon.

I didn't wait to see if he was going to continue. I slipped from my chair and closed the short distance between our seats, standing in front of him, and placing myself between his legs. I wound my arms around his neck as he lowered his eyes to some spot on the floor. His hand dropped to his knee but he made no move to touch me.

"Martin..." I tried to use the voice my dad used when he attempted to explain the unexplainable. It always made me feel safe and comforted; in fact, I repeated my father's words now because they seemed right for the situation and it was the best I could do.

"We can't change the past. But we can change how much importance we allow it to have over our future."

His lips tugged to the side and his eyes drifted shut. He shook his head slowly, but I was gratified when his hands settled on my hips.

"Who told you that?" he asked without opening his eyes; his tone told me he was reluctantly amused.

"My dad, when I didn't study for a trigonometry test in high school and then subsequently failed it."

Martin's laugh burst forth with a *tsk* and a wonderful scoffing noise; it was adorable because it sounded involuntary. Best of all, when he opened his eyes and gazed at me, he didn't appear to be angry.

He looked a little helpless, a little lost, a little hopeful, and a lot vulnerable.

"Oh, Martin." I stepped all the way forward and pulled him into a hug, which he returned immediately. I felt a surge of fierce protective-ness for my Martin. It took my breath away, caught me off guard.

My Martin...oh, sigh.

In that moment I hated his father—a man I'd never met—and his stepmother for their treatment of him. I hated them for being too blind or evil to recognize how sacred his heart was, how he needed tender-ness, care, and love. My heart broke a little as I wondered whether he'd ever experienced genuine affection from another person.

Given what I knew so far, I thought the chances were slim.

Yet, there was something about him that made me think he knew what *normal* was; he seemed to want normal for himself. He knew that mutual respect, honesty, and affection were essential, even though those closest to him had never demonstrated any of those character traits.

His enemies were now my enemies. I hoped he knew that, no matter what happened between us in the long run, whether we ended as friends after all this was over, he had a safe place with me.

After several wordless moments, I kissed his neck then spoke against the spot. "We have several strange conversations queued up for today's agenda, but for right now I say we just hug it out for a bit, then maybe go swimming."

He *tsk*-laughed again, a little longer this time, then pulled away so he could look at my face. I gave him a bright smile; my heart didn't hurt quite as badly now he was looking less lost.

"Also, I hope you brought food because I'm hungry." I patted his shoulders. "Please tell me there're cookies."

"Are you always like this?" he asked, his eyes narrowing in mock suspicion.

"Like what?" I pretended to be confused. "Amazing?"

"Yeah," he nodded, finally smiling, "amazing."

* * *

AT THE STERN of the boat, we ate at a table that popped up from the deck. Martin set some fishing poles up and left them in these neat fishing pole holders that buzzed when there was a bite, then reeled the fish in on the line. I didn't even know that kind of thing existed.

"You mean you don't have to hold the pole in order to fish?"

"Nope."

I felt slightly outraged. "But...that's the whole point of fishing, to hold the pole, to reel in the fish."

"The point of fishing is to catch fish."

"That's cheating. You're cheating at fishing."

He shrugged. "Outcome is the same."

A light breeze picked up his hair and tossed it about a bit, playing with it, as though the wind couldn't resist touching him. Behind Martin was the endless green-blue of the Caribbean and the endless, cloudless soft blue of the sky. The unmistakable, but not unpleasant, salty smell of seawater made the palette of greens and blues feel sharper somehow. Martin's gorgeous eyes almost glowed on his tanned face.

I smiled at him, because he'd just placed the last of the grapes from lunch on my plate. "Well, where did you even find this infernal contraption? At the lazy fisherman dot com?" I teased.

"No," he said, "but that's a good domain name. I invented it."

"What?"

He popped a grape into his mouth, chewed, then took a drink of his bottled water before finally answering. "The lazy fishing pole. I invented it."

I stared at him. I couldn't decide if I was outraged or proud.

"When did you do that?"

"It was my eighth grade science fair project. The first mock up was very crude since I'd built it myself. But I did a Kickstarter for it my junior year of high school and they're now manufactured in Switzerland."

"Oh." I didn't know quite what to say, so I studied the grapes.

He was so full of surprises. He was unexpected, and not at all who I thought he'd be. Yet at the same time, who he was made total sense. Martin seemed to really know himself, have a level of comfort and confidence in his own skin. This confidence was wrought by multiple trials by fire, and it manifested as not caring what anyone else thought.

I envied that. I envied him.

Everyone I met always presumed to know who I was because of who my family was, and therefore, what I would do with my life. I had huge, impressive, worthwhile shoes to fill—so obviously that's what I would do.

But rather than think about my own shortcomings, apropos of nothing, I blurted, "I don't think we should move in together."

Martin's hand stopped midair as he reached for another grape on my plate and his blue-green eyes told me I'd caught him off guard.

"Really..." he said, like he was stalling for words.

"First of all, Sam is counting on me. As well, I'm very regimented about things like dishes and messes and such. I wouldn't want us to be roommates and find that we can't stand living with each other. Sam and I keep a chore list and we're both really good about sticking to it. Would you be that kind of roommate? Also, there is the matter of cost, size, and personal taste. I don't mind living in a small space, I actually kind of like it. I also like how inexpensive it is compared to an apartment. It's likely that where you'll want to live wouldn't suit my budget or my size preference. As well, the opposite is probably true..."

Martin watched me through my well-reasoned speech. His surprise at my subject choice changed to a leveling glare of cynicism, then frustratingly, complete withdrawal.

"If you don't want to move in with me you can just say so."

I wrinkled my nose at his frosty tone. "No, Martin—it's not about wanting or not wanting to move in with you, it's about thinking through all the pros and cons of any proposed action."

His jaw ticked. "Do you want to be with me after this week is over?"

"Yes. We're dating. We're officially two dating people who are dating each other, at least that is my understanding. We are dating, right?"

He nodded coolly, but said nothing.

I tried to pacify his sudden surly mood. "We don't have to move in together in order to be dating, or be in a relationship, or see each other."

"When?"

I frowned at his question because I didn't know what he was asking and he looked extremely frustrated.

"When what?"

"When are we going to be together? When will I see you when we get back?"

"You want specific dates and times?"

"How often? Will I see you every day? Or will it be once a week?"

"Martin—"

"Maybe we should make a chore chart for it." He stood abruptly, looking menacing and angry. "Then you can allocate just the right amount of time to maintaining an adequate relationship."

I stood as well, heat spreading from my chest to my neck. "That's not how it would be."

"I'm going for a swim." Martin turned from me and pulled off his shirt; he shook off his sandals as I rounded the table, trying to reach him before he jumped off the boat.

"You're overreacting. Just stop for a second and think about this. I know if you think about this you'll see that I'm right."

Martin's attention was on his watch as he removed it from his wrist. "All I know is that I'm completely crazy about a girl who doesn't want to move in with me because she's worried I'll be messy."

"That's an oversimplification of the issue, Martin Sandeke. You can't let your passion make every decision for you."

"No, you're right." He stilled and glanced up at me then, his eyes glinting like daggers, his voice hard. "It's much better to be a musical prodigy, to love something passionately, but give up and *bow out gracefully*. To not fight. To talk yourself out of caring about what matters to you, because then you'll have all those fine deeds and reasonable decisions and logic to keep you warm at night."

My mouth moved but nothing emerged. He was being completely crazy and irrational and I had no idea how to interact with someone who was being completely crazy and irrational.

But then I looked at him more closely as he placed his watch on the table and saw the unhappy curve of his mouth. I realized I'd hurt him.

"Martin." I placed my hand on his bicep to stay his movements. He winced a little at the contact, but I took heart in the fact he didn't shrug me off. "I'm not trying to hurt you. I just want us to be—"

"Smart," he finished for me, his resentful gaze softening as it moved over my face. "I know. You always want to be smart and do the right thing. But the problem is, Parker…I just want you."

[7]

COVALENT BONDING AND ORBITAL OVERLAP

M ARTIN WENT FOR a swim. A really, really long swim. I was a little jealous of the water.

I distracted myself by finishing up my last term paper.

He returned and I tried to keep from gawking or drooling as he pulled himself onto the boat. He was wet, so very, very wet. As such, all the oxygen seemed to abruptly disappear from the atmosphere. He dried himself off and I pretended not to watch. Eventually, mostly dry, he disappeared into the captain's cabin.

I sighed unhappily then distractedly studied for my math test. Then I heard a strange buzzing and clicking and realized it was coming from Martin's infernal lazy fishing pole contraption.

He'd caught two yellowfin tuna by proxy and I had to make a split decision: I could go get him and risk losing both fish, or I could try to haul up the smaller, more manageable of the two. I was successful in bringing up the one, but the other broke loose and swam off in the three minutes it took to get my fish netted, unhooked, and deposited in a huge cooler of sea water set on the deck.

"You're pretty good at that."

I looked over my shoulder and found him leaning against the doorway to the upper deck cabin, watching me as I bent over the cooler and untangled the fish from the net. He was still shirtless and droplets of water were clinging to his hair.

"I lost the bigger fish." I straightened and said this apologetically. "I didn't think I could bring it up by myself and I didn't want to lose them both."

He shrugged and moved away from the door, walking to me until he crowded my space. His hands slipped under my T-shirt and caressed the expanse of my stomach.

"Hi," he said, looking down at me. He looked a little cagey and regretful.

"Hi," I said, then lifted on my tiptoes to give him a kiss. It was just a soft press of my mouth to his, but I needed it. When I went back on my feet I saw he needed it too.

"I'm sorry," he said.

"You're forgiven," I said.

He smiled, and those thorny feelings in his gaze gave way to relief. "I haven't told you why I'm sorry."

"You're still forgiven."

His thumbs dipped into the waistband of my shorts, rubbing down the line of my hips. "I did overreact. And all your points are valid ones. I just don't want to get back to campus and for this to go away. I need to see you, often."

I wound my arms around his back and pressed him to me. Really, I wanted to feel his skin against mine, but for now I decided to settle for just his warmth.

"This isn't going away. I don't think I'm going to disappear into a chemistry lab cabinet when we get back. And besides, if I did, you'd know where to find me." I kissed his collarbone. Damn he was delicious. Being so close to him had my hormones throwing a parade and making a Slip 'n Slide out of my pants. It would have been embarrassing if I'd cared, but I didn't. I'd grown to love the way he made me feel.

"Promise me that when we get back, maybe in a month, or when finals are over, you'll reconsider moving in together."

The idea of dating Martin—or still dating Martin—during finals made what we were doing here feel very real, and it gave it a sudden gravity. It was a fixed time point in the future. I thought about meeting him for study sessions in the library and coffee shop. How it would be. How he might spend the night with me on those odd weekends when Sam went home.

I realized, or understood better, why he wanted to move in together. If we shared an apartment our default would be together—like it had been here—and he didn't want to give that up. Neither did I.

"Where are you living over the summer?" I asked, smoothing my hands up and down his back just so I could feel more of him.

"I was already planning to move out of the house in April. I was thinking of an apartment downtown."

"So far away?"

"Yeah, but then I can catch the train to New York easier."

"What's in New York?"

He hesitated for a minute, watched me, and his hands stilled. "A project I'm working on."

"What kind of project? A class assignment?"

He shook his head, his fingers moving around to the back of my shorts. "No. It's not for class. It's a...a venture capitalist thing."

My eyebrows bounced up and down as I oscillated between surprised and impressed. "Just a little venture capitalist thing, in New York?"

He huffed a laugh, his voice low, rumbly, and delicious as he said, "Yeah. Something like that."

"Does it have anything to do with your cheating fishing poles? Maybe a golf club that plays eighteen holes all by itself?"

"No, it has nothing to do with fishing. It's, uh, it's satellites."

"Oh." I nodded, made sure I looked like I thought satellites were as impressive as a finger painting. "Oh, satellites. Who *doesn't* have a little venture capitalist side project in New York about satellites? I have twenty at least."

He was full on chuckling now, looking at me like I was cute and hilarious. "Really? We should compare notes."

"How much money are you trying to raise for this little cosmic endeavor? Five? Ten million?" I'd thrown the figures out there because they sounded preposterous.

He shocked me by responding seriously, "Sixty and some change, but I have a way to raise the capital, so we're golden."

My mouth fell open and I struggled not to choke on my bewilderment. "Who *are* you? Why are you even going to college?"

"College is good for making contacts, meeting the right people— smart people who I might be able to employ later— and networking." He shrugged, like the college experience was one big social networking conference or a giant job interview for all of his classmates in the inevitable Martin Sandeke Empire. He added, "I also like to row and I like to win."

I couldn't help but tease him. "Am I one of your right people? Are you planning to employ me later?"

"No." He grew sincere, introspective, and his tone mimicked his expression. "You were a complete surprise and you might ruin everything." Then he added as a distracted afterthought, "You might ruin me."

I felt a little stab of sober hurt just under my heart. "I wouldn't," I implored, my fingers flexed into the muscles of his back. "Martin, I would never ruin you."

"You wouldn't do it on purpose," he soothed, looking resigned. "But you could if you wanted to."

"I won't want to."

He merely smiled wryly in response and let me look at him. Then he took advantage of me being distracted by reaching into my shorts and swimsuit and touching my bare skin.

"Let's go downstairs."

"Why?"

He bent to my jaw and kissed it, then kissed a path to my ear. "I want to do very bad things to this bottom." He growled, grabbing and massaging me, making my breath hitch and liquid heat race to very nice places…in my pants.

"What kind of things? Give me some details. Maybe a numbered list." I was teasing him but my voice betrayed me, as it was breathy and uneven.

He lifted his head from where he'd been biting me; his gaze was heated, hooded, and full of sexy promise.

"Let's get you naked and I'll show you."

* * *

I WAS NAKED. He was not.

He'd kept his swim shorts on all day, then changed into boxer briefs and pajama bottoms for bedtime.

I wasn't comfortable being naked in general. Over the course of my life I was only ever naked right before, during, or after bathing/a shower or changing into a bathing suit; therefore, being naked while alone with Martin specifically, felt like an epic skydive outside of my comfort zone.

I briefly wondered if this made me an odd duck. Did other nineteen-year-old girls—less sexually repressed girls—spend minutes and hours alone with themselves naked? Admiring their knees, becoming acquainted with their elbows, discovering the dots and indents of their backside? Somehow I doubted it, at least not girls from the United States of America.

This was the country where Janet Jackson's inadvertent boob exposure during the 2004 Super Bowl led many to believe it was a sign of the Apocalypse. Movies frequently displayed death, violence, and gore with a PG-13 rating, but *god forbid* a nipple be exposed, or an ass crack. Cuss and swear and maim and kill, but the sight of the human body is lascivious, offensive, and shameful.

Really, in the USA, there were only two sure ways one could ever see a human male penis without having sex: porn, and anatomy/physiology 101. Part of me wondered if zoos were so popular as a direct result, giving kids an opportunity to assuage their curiosity with animal anatomy, and therefore labeling the experience as educational.

Presently, I was naked and being spooned. Martin was spooning me. It felt very surreal and far-fetched, just like almost every other moment during this week. It was on the tip of my tongue to yell to no one in particular that I was snuggling with Martin Sandeke, as in: I AM SNUGGLING WITH MARTIN SANDEKE!

But instead I asked, all calm and cool, "So, tell me, do you prefer to be the spoon or the spooned?"

His lips were against my upper back, where my neck met my shoulders, and I felt his mouth curve into the barest smile. "I don't know, I've never done this before."

"What? Spooned?"

"Yeah."

I allowed this to sink in. Once it did, I grinned into the dim cabin and said with no small amount of wonder, "Kaitlyn Parker has popped Martin Sandeke's spooning cherry."

I felt his smile grow just before he said, "It's only fair. I hope to pop your forking cherry."

I sucked in a shocked breath, but then burst out laughing, half-heartedly covering my face. After a moment he joined in, and I felt his chest shake with laughter.

It felt good, talking to him, joking with him. I couldn't pinpoint when we'd grown to this level of comfort with each other, but it was a bit strange to think I'd let him touch my body with intimacy before I'd felt confident I could tease him about spooning.

We'd spent all day fooling around, then swimming, then eating, then talking, then fooling around some more. He liked me on my stomach, lying on the bed, his fingers between my spread legs, biting my back and sides and neck and bottom.

He also liked me straddling his face while he lay on the bed, his fingers digging into my hips and thighs while he tasted me.

He also liked me straddling his hips while we just made out like hormone-addled teenagers, necking, touching, and petting, learning each other's sweet spots.

Despite how the day had started, I admitted to myself that it had quickly ascended to one of my favorite days of all time. I felt happy. *So happy.* Giddy, excited, joyful, thrilled, and carefree in a way I'd never felt before. Just lying with him was exhilarating. We were a team and I felt certain I could rely on him, and I wanted him to rely on me.

"That, sir," I referred to his forking joke, "was hilarious and well timed. You win today's Witty Wednesday contest."

"I didn't know we were having a contest, and I thought today was Wet-and-Wild Wednesday."

"A Wednesday can be more than one thing, it doesn't just have to be wet and wild. It can also be witty, or wistful, or worrisome. That's the beauty of Wednesdays."

"What did I win? What's my prize?"

"Just the knowledge you've won, and that you have my respect."

He squeezed me. "How many people have your respect?"

I thought about this, my lips twisting as my eyes narrowed. "Forty-seven...and a half."

"Who is the half?"

"It's not a half, it's two three-fourths, and they belong to John F. Kennedy and Richard Nixon. I three-fourths respect them."

"You respect historical figures?"

"Yes, after careful vetting."

"Richard Nixon? Really?"

I nodded. "Yes. He did a lot to normalize our relationship with China. As well he pulled us out of Vietnam. But then...the whole power-hungry arrogance, lying, and being too much of a dweeb to wear makeup on TV stuff brings him down to three-fourths."

"And JFK? What were his deficiencies?"

"I don't like how he treated women, especially his wife. He didn't practice what he preached and that made him slimy. Also, the Bay of Pigs fiasco and groupthink, *ugh*. Don't even get me started."

"Okay, I won't get you started." He squeezed me again.

"How about you? How many people do you respect?"

Martin sighed. I felt his exhale against my neck as it sent several of my hairs dancing over my shoulder, tickling me.

"Let's see," he stalled.

"Too many to count?"

"Five...no, four."

"Four? Only four?"

"Yes."

"Well, who—pray tell—are these pillars of humankind?"

"Unlike you, historical figures don't have my respect, not actively anyway. If I've never met a person I can't respect them."

"You sound so serious."

"It is serious."

"Now I really want to know." I shifted my legs and turned my head so I could peer at him over my shoulder.

"You, of course."

I smiled, but then quickly suppressed it. "Of course."

He still appeared serious as he continued, "Eric."

"Your teammate?"

He nodded.

I turned my head back to my pillow, pleased to hear that Martin respected Eric since I was pretty sure Sam really, really liked Eric.

"And my business partner."

"For the satellite venture capitalist thing in New York?"

"Yes."

"Who is the fourth?"

"Your mother, Senator Parker."

I frowned, blinked rapidly several times, my tone betraying my surprise. "My mother? You've met my mother?"

I felt him nod as his arms tightened around my torso.

"Martin, when did you meet my mother?"

"Three years ago, in Washington, DC."

"What...how...when?" Unable to settle on a question, I turned completely around so I could see his face. "Okay, start from the beginning. What happened? How did you meet her?"

He shrugged like the fact he'd met my mother *before* he'd met me was not a big deal. "I was in DC with my father. We were at a restaurant having lunch with a team of telecom lobbyists, and your mother walked in with a few members of her staff."

"And you respect her because...she ordered the hamburger instead of a salad?" I squinted at him, trying to understand how one brief encounter with my mother three years ago could garner his respect, how she could become one in a short list of four.

"My father stopped her as she walked past, suggested that she join us for lunch." Martin's gaze moved to a place over my shoulder, his eyes unfocused as he recalled the scene. "It was the first time I'd seen my father be polite to *anyone*. And she looked at him like he was scum." The side of his mouth ticked upward at the memory.

"What did she say? Did she have lunch with you?"

He shook his head and smiled softly. "No. She said, '*No, thank you,*' and tried to walk away; but he stepped in her path and pushed her about it. Then she said, '*I'd rather eat glass than suffer through one second of your corrupt and tedious company.*'"

Martin's smile grew as his eyes shifted back to mine.

"Holy rude comeback, Batman!" I exclaimed on an exhale.

"I know. And she was fierce, in control, cold even. She made him look small and insignificant by comparison." He said this like he admired her, how she'd cut down his father. "After lunch I found out who she was, looked up her voting record, and then it all made sense."

"How so?"

"Because she's the chairwoman of the Commerce, Science, and Transportation Committee in the senate. She's sponsored or co-sponsored every pro-consumer and anti-Big Telecom bill that's been drafted in the last ten years."

I felt the need to defend her. "That's because telecom companies in the US hold a monopoly and enter into informal non-compete agreements with each other to keep prices artificially high, which means no one can ever get Sandeke Telecom, or Brighthouse, or Version to actually provide competitive rates let alone appropriate customer service. Is it too much to ask for reasonable Internet speeds that cost less than $100 a month? Or a service call window that doesn't span eight hours? Who has time for that?!"

Martin chuckled, grabbing my wrists; I hadn't realized it but I'd started gesturing with my hands to demonstrate my frustration.

"I know, I know. I agree," he said, trying to pacify me, rubbing the inside of my arms and kissing me softly. "Your mother does good work in Washington."

She did. I knew she did. She was amazing and I loved that my superhero mother was on his short list. He had exceptionally good taste.

Regardless of our agreement on her awesomeness, I squinted at him again, pursing my lips. "It feels weird talking about my mother while I'm in bed with you."

"Then what do you want to talk about?"

I blurted the first thing that came to mind, "What was Martin Sandeke like as a kid?"

He lifted an eyebrow in response. "Talking about your mother is weird, but talking about me as a kid isn't?"

"Just answer the question."

Martin considered me for a moment before responding. "I was...quiet."

"So you were a watcher."

"A watcher?"

"You were one of those creepy kids who watched the other kids play."

"I wasn't creepy."

"I was. I was a creepy watcher. I watched the other kids play—quite creepily—and tried to make sense of their games. Mostly the girls. They seemed to do a lot of fighting with each other. And crying. And making up. And whispering."

"But you didn't?"

"No." I remembered how it had hurt at first, being snubbed when I was seven and eight and eleven and sixteen, but then my mother told me I shouldn't waste energy on average people because they would never amount to anything beyond ordinary. *"You don't need to befriend them in order to lead them,"* she'd said.

I continued, pushing away the memory. "They didn't let me play their reindeer games, mostly because I was creepy, but also because I was always trying to make them stop fighting. I tried to make lasting

88

peace. But encouraging harmony between little girls is like trying to negotiate a Middle East peace treaty."

Martin exhaled a laugh and tucked a strand of hair behind my ear and shoulder. "I wanted everyone to get along and they just wanted to be dramatic. But that was okay. Their rebuffs allowed me to perfect the art of hiding at a very young age."

"Why did you hide? Did they make fun of you?"

I shook my head. "No. They ignored me. I think I hid because hiding made it my choice. You can't be ignored if no one can see you." I was talking from a stream of consciousness, having never really thought about why I hid before. The revelation of my motivations made me feel acutely uncomfortable, so I cleared my throat and changed the subject. "What were you really like as a kid? Other than quiet?"

"Stubborn."

"Ha! I'm shocked." Then I added under my breath, "I'm lying. I'm not shocked."

Martin pinched my rib, just enough to make me squirm. "I was quiet, stubborn, and shy."

"Shy?" I settled into the mattress, my cheek on his arm, and frowned at this last adjective. "I cannot imagine you being shy."

"Why? Because I'm so outgoing now?"

I thought about this—a shy Martin—as my eyes searched his, thought about his behavior for as long as I'd known him.

He'd barely spoken to me as my lab partner, though he'd apparently been thinking about me for quite a while. I remembered the time he'd asked for my phone number last semester and how he wouldn't look me in the eye while he spoke. At the time I thought it was arrogance. I recalled that at the party last Friday he'd been upstairs playing pool instead of downstairs getting drunk and engaging in merriment.

This prompted me to think and ask at the same time, "Martin, do you like parties?"

His eyes narrowed, but he said nothing.

My eyes widened, and I proclaimed, "You don't like parties! You sneak!"

He caught my wrists before I could do anything—like tickle him or pull away or smack his shoulder—and he brought my hands to his bare chest.

"No. I don't like parties."

"Then why did you make me go?"

"Because I liked the idea of showing you off as my date."

My nose wrinkled. "That makes no sense."

"I didn't say it made sense, it just is."

Now my eyes crinkled. "But you left me when we arrived."

"We've already been over this. I left to show you I wasn't going to…what did you call it? Pee on you? I looked for you twenty minutes later and couldn't find you. You went and hid in the laundry room. Instead of showing you off as my date, I spent half the night trying to find you."

"Is that why you were so pissed when you found me?"

"No. I was pissed before I found you, because I thought you might have gone off with someone else. I was relieved when I found you, but then pissed because you preferred to read a book over being with me."

"Poor, poor Martin." As much as I could with him holding my wrists, I petted his chest. "I will kiss your ego and make it better."

He lifted a single eyebrow. "I don't want you to *kiss* it."

I flattened my lips and blinked at him once, very slowly. "Are you always thinking about sex?"

"Yes."

I snorted.

"More accurately, sex with you."

I stilled, and watched him as he watched me. Before, when he'd joked about *popping my forking cherry,* it had felt like a joke. But now…not so much.

I didn't think I was ready for that, not yet. We'd been together less than a week. I'd given him my trust less than three days ago. This might have been dating boot camp, but I was still trying to wrap my mind around the concept of passion. Having sex with Martin before it was making love to Martin would be a bad idea.

I didn't want to confuse one with the other.

90

"Martin, I don't—"

"I know. You're not ready yet." He nodded, his eyes darting between mine, his body shifting closer in a deliciously lithe movement as one of his hands released my wrist and smoothed down the length of my body, from my shoulder to my hip.

Then, making me both smile and scowl, he added, "Maybe tomorrow."

[8]

TRANSITION METALS AND COORDINATION CHEMISTRY

T HURSDAY MORNING DAWNED and I found myself one half of a tangled mass of limbs. In Martin's defense, I was totally crowding his side of the bed. I was basically sprawled on top of him.

Aaaaand, I was still naked.

Diffused sunlight filtered through the undersea portals; I had no idea what time it was. I disentangled myself from Martin, careful not to wake him, and went about getting dressed and making breakfast. Then I took a cup of coffee up to the deck and studied for my upcoming math test, feeling all warm and fuzzy and happy with life in general, especially and specifically because of the sexy boy downstairs.

Martin joined me sometime later, bringing me a new, hot cup of coffee. Wordlessly, he gave me a toe-curling kiss good morning—even though it was already afternoon—and, looking smug and satisfied by my breathlessness, took the chair across from mine. He opened his laptop and began working on something or other, likely something serious and important and poised to make him millions.

We didn't talk. We sat together in companionable silence. It was... really great. Comfortable and easy. Every once in a while I'd catch him watching me. He would smile his pleased smile when our eyes met, but he'd never look away.

I began to daydream about what life would be like if I did agree to move in with Martin, and that was dangerous because smart Kaitlyn knew it was too hasty. But silly, prematurely falling in love Kaitlyn wanted to doodle our names together on notebooks and take cooking classes together on weekends.

Maybe he would come see me play my jam sessions on Sunday nights. Maybe I'd take the train and meet him in New York for lunch on days when I didn't have class. Maybe I'd write songs for him and about him. Maybe we'd sleep together every night, having fun and taking comfort in each other's bodies. Maybe he'd sleep naked too at some point.

But I was only nineteen, and college wasn't a networking conference for me. I didn't know who I was or what I wanted to do with my life. I suspected that music was going to have to be a major part of it—not because I believed I was a prodigious talent, but because something had shifted within me on Tuesday night, and I couldn't stop thinking about it.

Whether I was good or magnificent or merely adequate didn't matter. I recognized music as a passion, one that I'd been repressing. Of course, I hadn't given the matter, the how and when, enough thought yet. I still had a great deal to sort through.

The idea of falling in love with Martin (if I hadn't already) before I had my head on straight about what I wanted to do and who I was made me feel uneasy. He was always going to be the alpha of his pack, as he didn't know any other way. I didn't want to get lost, lose myself before I'd been found, in his flock of admirers.

I was staring at him, lost in my ruminations, but didn't realize I was staring until he asked, "Hey, everything okay?"

I blinked him back into focus, and shook my head to clear it. "Uh, yeah. Fine."

He studied me, looked like he wanted to ask or say something. Eventually he did. "What do you think, Kaitlyn?"

"About what?" I gave him a friendly smile as I closed my note-book. I couldn't study anymore; there was no use pretending.

"About us."

I flinched involuntarily because his question was almost eerily attuned to my current musings; I wondered tangentially if—in addition to everything else—Martin Sandeke was a mind-reader.

I looked away from him and studied the horizon. It was another beautiful day.

"I think we're having a lot of fun."

He was quiet and I felt his eyes on me. The silence didn't feel quite so comfortable anymore.

Then, very softly, he asked, "What's going on in your head?"

Out of nowhere and as a consequence of nothing, I said, "I'm afraid of letting everyone down."

He paused for a beat then asked, "What do you mean?"

"My eighth grade science fair project was a solar heater and it was made out of tin foil, black paint, and a shoe box."

"So?"

"So," I returned my gaze to his, "I'm never going to be a great scientist or a world leader."

He watched me like he was waiting for me to continue. When I didn't, he prompted again, "So…?"

"So? So?! You said it yourself yesterday to that vile woman. I'm Kaitlyn Parker; my grandfather is an astronaut; my dad is the dean of the college of medicine at a very excellent medical school; my grandmother outfitted the first nuclear submarines with freaking nuclear weapons; my mother might be the first female president of the United States in the next ten years…and I'm not brilliant."

He laughed. At first it was a short laugh of disbelief. Then it became a full on belly laugh when he saw I was serious. He was wiping tears from his eyes and shaking his head.

"It's not funny," I said, even though I fought a smile. Of course, it was funny; and I didn't mind laughing at myself.

I was smart. I knew that. I had no reason to complain. I came from a loving—if not comparatively regimented and sterile—family. I had all my fingers and toes. I had everything to be grateful for.

And yet…

I knew who I was supposed to be, but I was not that person. As well, I had no idea who I actually was.

When he finally stopped laughing, he sat back in his chair and considered me with glittering eyes over steepled fingers. A warm smile lingered over his features.

"Kaitlyn, you are very intelligent, and besides that you're a musical prodigy."

I shook my head. "I know you know what I mean, and I didn't say what I said because I was fishing for compliments—though, if I were fishing for compliments, I would want one of your cheating fish pole holders."

His smile widened, though he persisted the point. "Why do you think you have to be a scientist or a world leader? Why not focus on your music instead?"

I glared at him. "Come on, Martin. Don't play dumb. You know it's what everyone expects. I may love music, but aren't there enough musicians in the world? If I have even the smallest talent or aptitude for politics or scientific endeavors, and the connections, don't I owe it to society to at least try?"

"What other people expect doesn't matter. You don't owe society anything. Screw society! You should do what makes you happy."

"That's ridiculous. Life isn't about making yourself happy. Life is about exploiting your talents for humanity, in order to make lasting difference for good when and where you can, and for as long as you are able."

"Is this one of your stupid life rules?"

"Don't call them stupid. My life rules keep me from making avoidable mistakes."

"What a load of self-sacrificing, martyring bullshit."

"It is not! There is great value in self-sacrifice."

"And you think you can't 'do good' with music?"

"No. Not as much as I could by stepping up and becoming a leader like my mother or a scientist like my grandmother. Even you respect my mother."

"Yeah, but I don't want to fuck your mother."

I felt a spike of anger at his crass reply. "Are you telling me that who my family is has nothing to do with why you like me? That it doesn't make me very attractive girlfriend material?"

He held my glare and his grew increasingly heated, the earlier amusement giving way to stony severity. He took his time answering, like he was debating with himself, and eventually his non-answer seemed to speak for itself.

I felt abruptly hot and cold and adrift.

"Martin…?"

"Of course not, Parker," he finally said.

I exhaled my relief, but the back of my neck tingled. Something about the way he was looking at me, how long it had taken him to respond, didn't feel honest.

"You misunderstand my meaning." His tone was firm, unyielding, like he was trying to lead me to a certain conclusion. "I meant, of course I'd never tell you that who your family is has nothing to do with why I like you so much, because that statement would be a lie. Who your family is has a great deal to do with why you're very attractive girlfriend material. Of course I want you because of who your family is."

My hesitant relief became stunned incredulity at his admission. He was watching me closely, though giving none of his own thoughts away.

I stood abruptly, filled with sudden restless energy, and a fierce need to reject his words. My hands came to my hips, then fell to my legs, then pushed through my hair. Stunned incredulity grew into a cauldron of boiling anger.

"How can you say that to me? You know better than anyone, better than *anyone* else, what it's like to be wanted because of who your family is."

"Because it's true," he answered, watching me carefully.

"What? This is…"

…you are the Olympic gold medal and the Nobel Peace Prize and the Pulitzer Prize and the Academy Award of marriage material. Ray's irritating words from Monday came back to me in a rush

accompanied by the thundering sound of blood rushing between my ears.

Distractedly, I said, "Ray warned me about this."

"Ray?" This got his attention, he sat up straighter.

"Yes. Ray." I glanced at Martin, feeling equal parts anger and confusion. "He said that you liked me because of my credentials, that I was the girl guys like you married after you finished sowing your poison oats—or some such nonsense—but it wasn't nonsense because he was right. He was right." I muttered this last statement to myself.

"He was right," Martin confirmed, again stunning me. This time the wind truly was knocked from my lungs.

"No, he wasn't." I shook my head, making the denial on his behalf because I didn't want it to be true.

"Kaitlyn, Ray was right. He knows what kind of girl I want, what I've been looking for."

I felt like he'd slapped me across the face or sucker-punched me in the stomach. Therefore, I didn't think much about the next words out of my mouth.

"You, Martin Sandeke, are a complete and total jerk-face! How dare you... How dare you! Why would you...and I thought..." I screamed this at him in fits and starts, which felt weird because I'd never screamed at anyone before in my life.

I decided just to go with it.

The line of his mouth became contemplative as he looked at me, but he said nothing. This only served to increase my frustration.

"What the heck is wrong with you?" I continued my tirade. "Aren't you going to defend yourself? Or are you just going to sit there and stare at me?"

"Do you want me to defend myself?"

"Yes!" I immediately responded, loudly and on instinct, the single-word admission ripped from some insurmountable desire to be wanted and seen for who I was, even if I didn't know who that person was yet.

"Why?" He was on the edge of his seat and his gaze was filled with a strange hope.

"Because..." My voice cracked and so did my heart. Stupid tears flooded my eyes.

Tuesday night's crying was cathartic, necessary, and I'd embraced it. But I didn't want to cry now. I didn't want to show weakness to someone who, by his own admission, cared more about who my family was than who I was as a person.

I kept thinking, *I knew it! I knew he would make me cry! Stupid Kaitlyn. Stupid passion. Stupid trust. Stupid jerk-face Martin Sandeke.*

I turned away from him before he could see my face crumble. I needed to hide. The desire was brutal. Thus, I tried to bolt for the cabin below deck, with my ultimate goal one of the two closets. But, somehow detecting my intentions, Martin had other plans. I listened to his chair hastily scrape against the deck, his quick steps circle the table.

He was hot on my heels as I descended the stairs and he intercepted me before I could grab for the handle of the closet door.

Martin gripped my shoulders and he turned me to face him.

"Let me go!"

"Christ, Kaitlyn. Calm down for a minute. You wanted me to defend myself, so listen."

"I hate you!" I yelled this, but I didn't really mean it. Besides feeling wonderfully dramatic and perfect in the moment, I wanted to hurt him. Because I was hurting.

"No, you don't. You're falling in love with me." He looked stunned by my outburst, but sounded almost pleased by it, like my reaction was part of some big plan, a game of strategy he'd been playing.

Damn it all, he was such a bully. I knew this, but I must have forgotten it someplace between his mouth and his hands and his eyes and his words.

I responded to this accusation through clenched teeth, sounding not at all convincing. "No, I'm not."

I fought his grip and pushed against his granite chest. Of course this did nothing but make him change his hold so I couldn't continue hitting him.

"Listen to me, Kaitlyn. Just—would you listen?"

I took a deep breath and forced myself to calm down.

Even though you don't feel calm doesn't mean you can't be calm.

I stilled. I closed my eyes so I couldn't see him. I needed to distance myself. I needed to either reason or bluff my way through this. My urge to cry dissipated as I thought through my action plan.

I would...I would just freeze him out. I could do that. I'd been doing it for months before he found me in that science cabinet and everything went to hell.

I cleared my throat, testing the steadiness of my vocal chords. "I changed my mind. I'm not interested. I don't care."

He laughed at this, though it sounded completely frustrated. "Shutting me out, are you? How convenient that you're able to just turn your feelings off so easily."

I kept my eyes shut and repeated over and over, *even though you don't feel calm doesn't mean you can't be calm.*

I had no reason to answer him, so I didn't. I just pretended he wasn't there. Eventually he'd have to let me go. When I was eleven, I spent seven hours in a closet waiting for a babysitter to leave. I didn't like her because she cheated at Monopoly.

Martin hadn't cheated at Monopoly, but he did just admit that he was using me because of who my family was. In some sick way it made sense. By his own admission, college was one large-scale job interview of his classmates for the future Martin Sandeke conglomerate. Why wouldn't he also be interviewing girls for the role of girlfriend?

In the game of life this made him one of my least favorite people. *He* was manipulating me. The very thing he detested in others. He knew I was falling in love with him. *He knew.* Was I the first girl he was going to *test*? Martin Sandeke's Girlfriend 1.0?

"You are so stubborn." Now he sounded upset. "Open your eyes and look at me."

I didn't. Instead I built the case against him in my mind. Everything he'd said and done became damning evidence and I felt myself grow numb.

"Fine. We'll do it this way."

Martin's hold changed, and he was walking me backward. The high mattress of the cabin's double bed hit my bottom and before I quite understood what was happening, he lifted me into his arms and placed me on the bed.

I did open my eyes then, scrambling away from him to the far corner of the mattress. I glared at him, hoped to communicate that I would kill him dead if he touched me with intent to arouse.

He seemed to understand the silent threat because he lifted his hands up and said, "I'm not going to touch you, not if you don't want me to. I'm just going to sit here, on this side. But you have to promise me that you won't cover your face or close your eyes again. I need you to see me when I say this. And I need to see you."

I said nothing. I wasn't going to make him any promises.

He paused, indulging himself in a moment to examine my face. At length, he said, "You're so good at that. You'll have to teach me how to do that, hide in plain sight. It's a handy skill." These words were surprisingly bitter, approaching the intersection of sarcasm and spite.

I pulled my knees up to my chest, wrapped my arms around my legs, and said nothing. Though I got the distinct impression he was stalling. I briefly wondered why, but then became irritated with myself for my curiosity. I shouldn't care.

He sat on the edge of the bed in the opposite corner, facing me. His features were hard, verging on resentful.

Abruptly, he released a breath and with it the words, "I'm in love with you, Kaitlyn."

I said nothing, but I did flinch. As silent seconds ticked by, feelings welled within me, ballooning past the numbness, and I could barely contain it. I felt like I was being stretched beyond my capacity, my chest tight and heavy, my stomach intermittently twisting and pitching. I was dizzy.

As well, I found I couldn't quite hold the enormity of his gaze paired with his admission, so earnestly spoken. I believed him and I couldn't quite handle this truth, so I removed my eyes from his and swallowed. It didn't help. I was shaking.

He cleared his throat, politely ignoring my turmoil, and said, "Who your family is, it's a part of you. Just like my family—all their fucked-up spite and bullshit—is also a part of me. We've been shaped by them but they don't define us. I'm not them. I don't have to be like them. You're not your illustrious ancestors. You don't have to be like them. You can be whoever you want. Our families couldn't be more different, but—because of who your family is—you understand what it means to have…expectations. To have people prejudge you or want to use you for who they are, what they've done, and what they have. That's what I meant when I said who your family is has a great deal to do with why you're very attractive girlfriend material."

I slid just my eyes to his. They were stinging and I felt like crying. I was overwhelmed but I was unable to keep from surveying him to discern the veracity of his words. He appeared to be completely sincere and I felt the gravity of his blue-green gaze to my bones.

Before I could catch myself, I blurted, "So you like me because I can empathize with you?"

"No…yes, that's definitely part of it, but…" His frustration was a tangible thing, curling around his strong body and filling the air with tension. "I *like* you because you are Kaitlyn—genuine, beautiful, brilliant, amazing Kaitlyn—not because you're Kaitlyn Parker. And I'm *in love* with you because I can't help myself."

Oh well…barnacles.

That struck me right in the feels.

I knocked my feels on their collective swooning asses for a moment because I needed to focus on the real issue. "But, upstairs you were trying to make me think you were using me. Why make it sound like you were just using me?"

He leaned forward, but made no move to advance closer, his voice rising with every word. "Because you're so controlled all the time. I ask you to move in with me and you make a pro/con list, as though we'd be *just* roommates, but make no reference to what you feel for me, like it doesn't factor. I'm in love with you and I have no idea what you feel for me, if you feel anything at all!"

"How can you say that? How can you even think it? Who was upstairs yesterday giving you a hug and trying to comfort you after your wicked stepmother showed up?"

"You. You were upstairs." His tone held a hard edge, ripe with unhappiness. "But you would have done that for anyone; you would have tried to make things right for any random person. I don't want to be just anyone to you."

I couldn't believe this. I couldn't believe him. "Then who has been on this boat with you since yesterday morning? Who was all up in your junk yesterday afternoon? And who woke up naked, tangled up with you this morning in this bed? You are not any random person to me! I've never done anything with anyone before! I've never let anyone so close. And these things, all these things we've been doing, and not just the physical stuff, the sharing of...of myself, of our dreams and our fears, this means something to me. None of this has been done lightly."

"I needed to be sure."

I hoped I was misunderstanding him somehow, because the alternative was completely cray-cray.

"So, help me understand this. Earlier, on the deck, just now...you misled me as some kind of test? To see if I'd be upset?"

"Yes." He nodded, looking unrepentant.

My brain was going to explode.

"That's messed up, Martin. You know this is a sore spot for me, if not *the sorest spot.* Your need for certainty does not matter more than my feelings. You don't purposefully hurt people you care about. You can't do that. That's not allowed!"

He flinched and abruptly stood, turned away, like he couldn't stand looking at me with the knowledge that he'd hurt me. He tugged his fingers though his hair and sighed, stalking back and forth from one side of the cabin to the other.

"I never wanted to hurt you. I didn't think I *could* hurt you. I didn't expect you to freak out like you did. You never freak out about anything. I just wanted to see how you would react. I wanted to see if I mattered."

"Well, looks like you have your answer. You matter. Happy now?"

"No. I'm the opposite of happy," he yelled back, then exhaled like he was out of steam. His gaze moved over me with such raw longing that I couldn't stand looking at him anymore. I closed my eyes *and* I covered my face.

A moment later I heard something crash followed by, "God*dammit!*"

I jumped at the sound and blasphemy, but kept my face buried. I was all mixed up and not one thought or feeling seemed to rise to the top.

"Kaitlyn, will you look at me?"

I gathered a fortifying breath then peeked at him between my fingers. It was the best I could do.

He was now glaring at me, likely irritated by the hands still covering my face.

Then he broke the stony silence. "I'm sorry," he said, then waited like he expected me to respond in a certain way, like we were following some script I hadn't been given. He growled impatiently, "So?"

"So what?"

"So, am I forgiven?"

My hands dropped from my face in my shocked outrage. "No!"

"What?" He was surprised.

How can he possibly be surprised?! Gah!

"What you did was not okay. You just purposefully hurt me as some dysfunctional litmus test." I scrambled off the bed and pointed at him, then waved my finger through the air to indicate his entire body. My face was screwed up in anger. "You're not forgiven, mister. Not by a long shot."

He turned and fell back on the bed. He groaned. He covered his face with his hands then rubbed furiously. "Tell me what I'm supposed to do and I'll do it."

"Lots of begging," I blurted and crossed my arms. Now I was pacing the cabin. My mind was a jumble. He was either a sociopath or just really clueless about basic human decency.

He chuckled. It only sounded half frustrated. "I don't know how to beg."

"Figure it out."

He removed his hands from his face and lifted his head, his eyes trailing up then down my body. "You don't want me to beg because you know I'm not going to beg. You want something else."

"I guess you'll just have to keep apologizing until I'm ready to forgive you."

"What was I supposed to do? It's Thursday. We leave on Saturday morning. I only have one more day."

I waved my arms through the air and may have resembled a bird struggling to fly. I appealed to any shred of sanity within him. "You could have just asked me, you fucking asshole jerk-face!"

Whoa!

My brain was shocked by the curse words and how good and necessary they felt given the circumstance. Perhaps cussing had its time and place…

Martin looked surprised as well, but instead of focusing on my foul language, he said, "I tried to do that."

"Really? I don't remember you saying at any point today," I lowered my voice to mimic his, " '*Hey, so, I love you. Are you in love with me?*'"

He sat up and stared at me, then shocked the hell out of me by actually saying, "I love you, Kaitlyn. Are you in love with me?"

[9]

ORGANIC AND BIOLOGICAL CHEMISTRY

W E'D REACHED A stalemate after our big fight. I couldn't answer his question. He wouldn't let me hide in the closet.

But we'd also reached a ceasefire, which was a very good thing because we were at least ten miles from the island and were utterly alone, with each other, for the rest of the day.

As such, things became strained, but also exceedingly polite. We went back above deck, ate lunch in relative silence. I cleared the dishes while he washed them. *Please* and *Thank you* were used in excess. But not *You're welcome.* For some reason, through an odd silent accord, we'd both agreed that *You're welcome* was off limits. Instead I'd say, *No problem.* Or he'd say, *My pleasure.*

Strained politeness became complete silence as he focused on fishing—actually holding the pole!—and I laid a towel on the platform of the bow and pretended to read my book. Instead, I thought about the nuttiness of the last few days and hours and what I was going to do about it all.

It was weird being with Martin and not talking to him. Therefore, when the sun approached the horizon and Martin asked if I wanted to head to the cottage and meet up with Eric and Sam, or stay on the boat for the night, I surprised both him and me when I responded that I wanted to stay on the boat. I also asked that he call Sam and Eric and let them know our plans.

Even though we'd been gone since Wednesday morning, I didn't want to go to the cottage when he and I weren't on more than polite speaking terms. Tomorrow was our last day. There was too much left unsaid. Regardless of whether we returned as friends or as more than friends, I wanted us to be in a good place.

Martin needed a friend. He needed a safe place. I wasn't in love with him...*or maybe I am...or maybe I'm falling in love with him... I don't know! Gah!*

But he mattered to me. Once the urge to hide in the closet passed, I was determined we not abandon what we'd started. I wanted to see it through.

When he learned I wanted to stay the night on the boat, Martin's mood shifted. He became less stoically polite and more actually polite.

He touched base with Eric via a satellite phone and I spoke to Sam for about three minutes, just long enough to assure her I was perfectly fine and I'd see her tomorrow in the afternoon.

Then he asked if I wanted to go for a swim, and I said yes. So we did. I did my best to ignore his body, because it still put me in a state of duress and gave me lusty pants, and he did an admirable job of keeping his hands to himself.

I made a salad and he made sashimi for dinner from a second yellowfin tuna he'd caught during the day. I was super impressed he knew how to make sashimi from whole tuna until I realized it was just cutting up the pretty part of the fish. I'm lying. I was still impressed. He was really good with his knife.

I praised his fishing and fish-cutting prowess. As well, we found a topic that was perfectly safe to discuss - our chemistry assignment. Therefore, after dinner we spread out the chemistry text, my notes, divvied up the tabulations and analyses, and set to work.

That's right, ladies and gentlemen, mark this day on the calendar of your life. Martin Sandeke helped with the tabulations and analyses.

If anything says, *I'm sorry I hurt you earlier by making you think I was using you for your family because it didn't occur to me to just ask how you felt about me*, helping with laboratory tabulations and analyses will do the trick.

Of course, it helped that he could do the work in a fraction of the time it took me. Then, maybe as a peace offering or maybe because he found himself enjoying the task, Martin offered to finish my portion of the tabulations. I let him.

I stretched as I stood and glanced at the half moon in the sky and the gathering clouds. It looked like it was going to rain.

I cleared the table and did the dinner dishes while he finished our lab work. While rinsing suds off the plates I was struck by a peculiar sensation of melancholy and mourning.

Tomorrow was our last day.

It was hard to believe that Martin had found me hiding in a science cabinet just last week. It felt like a lifetime ago. And yet, the week had flown by. Everything was different. I was different. I wondered how it was possible to live one's life, week in and week out, with nothing of consequence occurring.

But then suddenly, over the course of seven days, my entire world shifted. Just seven days that could have been like any other seven days.

This really was relationship boot camp. Through this fight—or whatever it was we were in—I'd learned more about Martin, understood him better than I had during the first six days of the trip combined.

1. He was damaged in ways I might never understand.

2. He was used to getting what he wanted—whether that be information or acquiescence—through manipulation.

3. He was in love with me, or at least he thought he was.

4. He was willing to learn from his mistakes.

5. He didn't want to repeat his mistakes.

6. He feared rejection.

The last revelation made him very, very normal. The first two, however, were sources of extreme concern. Numbers four and five gave me hope.

But the third made me feel weak every time I remembered him saying the words. It made my heart swell, it made it hard to breathe, it made the Bunsen burner in my pants go on alert level one million, and it made me willing to forgive him for almost anything.

That was the truth of it. I wanted to forgive him. I wanted to trust him again. I did trust him before the fight, because he'd earned my trust with sincerity and honesty. I also wanted him to trust me enough to risk his heart without trying to tear mine out in the process.

"Hey."

I glanced over my shoulder. Martin was in the doorway to the kitchen, holding two glasses, watching me. I took both from him with a tight smile, and turned back to the sink. I washed them, rinsed them, set them on the towel to dry.

Then he said, "I'm sorry."

I nodded, giving him my profile and another tight smile. "I know."

He moved into the small kitchen and stood behind me. I felt his warmth at my back and braced for his touch, my body tensing in anticipation.

But then music started playing from what could only have been a cell phone speaker. The sound quality was not good, but not terrible. I recognized the song within the first ten notes.

"Stevie Wonder?" I asked, turning completely around and glancing at the cell phone Martin held in his hand.

He nodded then reached around to place it on the towel next to the two glasses I'd just finished washing. "I thought you might like some music."

"*Overjoyed.*" I said the name of the song, and I'm afraid I was looking at Martin like he had three heads—all still devastatingly handsome, but three nevertheless. "You like Stevie Wonder?"

He nodded, not touching me with anything other than his penetrating gaze. "Yeah. He's one of my favorites. I like to rock out to *Sir Duke* or *Superstition* when I run."

"You like Stevie Wonder," I repeated, this time as a statement, because it was so odd. Then I laughed my astonishment and covered my huge grin with my hand. "This might be one of my most favorite things about you, Martin Sandeke."

His lips twisted to the side with a sardonic smile, his eyelids lowering. He reached for my hand, revealing my grin, and threaded his fingers through mine. "Don't cover your mouth, it's one of my most favorite things about you."

Butterflies and dragonflies held conference in my stomach then fluttered to the four corners of my extremities. Everything felt dream-like, hazy—likely the effect of exploiting Stevie Wonder as a sound-track to this conversation—and I found myself leaning toward him, lifting my chin.

He brushed his lips against mine, then tasted me with his tongue. It wasn't enough, yet he didn't deepen the kiss.

Instead he whispered, "I love you, Kaitlyn."

He leaned away, his eyes burning into mine, like he wanted to make sure I'd heard him and that I understood.

He released my hand.

Then he turned and walked out of the kitchen, leaving me with Stevie Wonder telling me how he'd built his castle of love, just for two, though I never knew I was the reason.

* * *

I COULDN'T SLEEP.

Where last night sleeping with Martin had been wonderful and filled with conversations about everything, tonight it was weird. We weren't touching. Instead we were relegated to the two sides of the bed, lying on our sides away from each other.

I was pretty sure he wasn't asleep either.

This suspicion was confirmed when I heard him sigh, then mutter, "Fuck this shit," under his breath, then shift, reach for my body, and pull me across the great divide into his arms and against his chest.

I smirked into the darkness.

"I can't sleep with you and not touch you," he said by way of gruff, unapologetic explanation. "So if you don't want me to touch you then I can go sleep on the couch."

"No." I snuggled backward, into his embrace. "No, stay. It seems I can't sleep either unless you're touching me."

He gave me a rumbly grunt of acknowledgement, then we settled into the stillness and the gentle rocking of the boat. Feeling cozy and warm and safe, I was approximately a half minute from drifting off to dreamland when Martin whispered against my neck.

"Please, Kaitlyn… Don't punish me."

I stiffened, the words confusing and alarming. I turned in his arms because I had a fierce urge to see his face.

I searched his eyes in the dim light before I spoke, and found him both weary and guarded.

"Martin, I've told you before. I don't punish people. You can expect honesty from me."

He lifted his hand and brushed his knuckles against the side of my cheek, then pushed several strands of my hair over my shoulder, following the progress with his eyes. "You haven't forgiven me yet."

"No. I haven't. But that doesn't mean I'm punishing you. I promise, I'm actively working to forgive you. I just need time."

He nodded his understanding, his gaze on my shoulder. He was touching me there, his thumb tracing a circle on my skin.

Then he returned his eyes to mine, ensnared them. His gaze and voice were laced with challenge as he asked, "Will you let me…can I make you feel good?"

The butterfly and dragonfly conference was back in my stomach. My heart was banging like a gavel, calling the sexy meeting to order. I flexed my thighs then pressed them together in automatic response to his request, my lower belly twisting, hot and liquid, my nipples tightening into stiff peaks.

Yes, I wanted to say. *God, yes. Please.*

I didn't quite trust myself to speak as my heart lurched painfully toward the vicinity of his heart, so I said nothing. But then I was struck with sudden inspiration.

"No," I breathed, not really believing I'd turned him down, yet found the wherewithal to add, "but I'd like to touch you."

His eyes widened and his handsome mouth parted. Everything about him softened and it was clear he hadn't been expecting my request. Holding my breath, I sat up in the bed and peeled the covers off his chest then pulled them completely away.

I reached for the waistband of his pajamas and he, as though coming back to himself, suddenly gripped my wrists to stop my progress.

"What are you doing?"

"Touching you."

His jaw was tight, his eyes betraying his confusion.

"Why?"

"Because I like touching you." I shrugged.

"Kaitlyn," he growled. He looked like he was in pain. "Don't tease me."

I waited for him to really *see* me, and I hoped he saw my sincerity. I hoped I didn't have to make verbal promises. I hoped he'd just simply trust me.

Eventually, and with a shaking breath, Martin released my wrists, though he looked fierce, dangerous as he did so. The glint in his eyes again reminded me of a wounded animal. I knew I had him in a vulnerable position and that was a unique prospect for him.

I curled my fingers around the band of his pajamas again, one hand on either side of his hips, and pulled them down his legs. He helped by lifting his hips, though his eyes never left mine.

I tried to make my expression as unconcerned as possible, even though I had no idea what I was about to do. Trying to feign confidence, I moved my eyes to his middle and gazed upon his very long, thick, and remarkably shaped penis. It was an anatomy 101, textbook penis—very normal looking in the best way possible, just longer and thicker.

Therefore, I had no idea why the sight of it got me so excited. It was a penis. There was nothing special about this penis—excepting being longer and thicker than the average representation of penises everywhere—other than the person to which it was attached.

Inexplicably, I wanted to taste it.

I bent forward to do just this when Martin stopped my progress by gripping my shoulders.

"What the hell, Kaitlyn?"

I looked at him then his penis. It jumped. He growled.

"No," he said. "No, no, no." He leveraged his grip on my shoulders to pull me back to where I'd been lying on the bed just minutes prior. He climbed on top of me, pinning me down. "You're not going to do that."

"What? Why? Do you not like it?"

"Of course I like it! But you've never done it." He was hovering over me, naked, nearly yelling because I wanted to give him my first blow job.

"You think I'll suck?"

He blinked at me, stunned for a moment, then groaned. His forehead hit my shoulder and it was then I realized the double meaning of my words.

"Oh snap, sorry. Of course, you *hope* I'll suck."

He groaned again. "You're trying to kill me."

"No." I laughed, because I couldn't help it, wishing I could touch him but he was holding my wrists. "I'm not. I just...I just want to make you feel good."

He didn't lift his head. "Right. You want to give me a blow job after I made you feel like shit this afternoon, and you still don't forgive me for it. Because that makes sense."

I didn't want to tell him that the reason I hadn't forgiven him yet was because he obviously didn't trust *me*. Him not trusting me to put his penis in my mouth was evidence enough. I thought it was a truth universally acknowledged that all men love blow jobs, beer, and again, blow jobs. Who turns down a blow job? Martin Untrusting Sandeke, that's who.

I huffed. "Listen, Sandeke. I would like to place your very picturesque penis in my mouth. Yes or no?"

He groaned, buried his head in my neck, bit me.

I bent my head to the side reflexively, little waves of wonderfulness spreading through me originating from where his mouth loved and tortured my neck.

"Yes or no?" I squeaked.

He lifted himself up, planking above me. His erection pressed into my belly and I tried not to squirm because I knew that would likely set him off again.

"Why are you doing this to me?" His tone was subdued, but his eyes glared menacingly.

"Yes or no?"

He swallowed, his gaze moving in a deliberate trail from my eyes to my mouth, neck, then breasts.

"Fine," he said, and I could tell he didn't think I'd actually do it. "But you have to take your shirt off."

"Why?"

"Because I don't want you to swallow this time. If you swallow your first time you'll never go down on me again, because cum tastes nasty."

"And you know this how?"

"Girls tell me so. Lots and lots of girls."

Now he was just being crude, trying to push me away instead of giving me an opportunity to demonstrate I was trustworthy. But I was stubborn.

I lifted my chin and asked, "I still don't understand why I need to take my shirt off."

"Because I like seeing my cum on your beautiful tits."

If he was trying to freak me out, gross me out, or shock me, his words had the opposite effect. My lungs filled with fire and my breath hitched. I don't know what possessed me to do it, but I repeated the words he'd already used on me twice.

"Don't tease me," I whispered.

His eyes widened as they searched mine. I'd surprised him again. Wide eyed, mouth slightly parted, looking at me like I was a sexy alien creature, Martin released my wrists and lay back on the bed.

I sat up again, pulling my shirt off and arranging myself near his middle. His hands had balled into fists at his sides. I guessed this was a byproduct of trying not to touch me.

I bent forward and reached for his shaft with one hand, holding his erection still because it was jumping, straining as I came closer. I licked my lips, breathing on him, and he groaned. He sounded so tortured. I felt a desperate spike to ease his suffering so I opened my mouth and slid my lips and tongue over his penis, accepting him into my mouth, suckling him.

He cursed—a steady stream of panting expletives intermixed with my name.

I moved up and down, remembering a porn movie I'd watched with Sam last semester while eating seasonally appropriate pumpkin-spiced kettle corn. Sam spent twenty minutes critiquing the girl's fellatio technique. She'd even paused the video, stood up, walked to the TV, and used my yardstick as a pointer.

"See here," she'd said, indicating to the girl holding her own breast, "she should be using that hand to tickle his balls, the inside of his thighs, or the backs of his knees. What's it going to do on her breast? Nothing. That's a misuse of resources."

I tried to recall the rest of her pointers, and knew that if I tried to bring him in too deep then I would gag. I wasn't ready for that yet, gagging being something I didn't enjoy, so I tried to focus on doing what felt good to me, what I enjoyed.

I was surprised and not surprised to learn that what I enjoyed, he also seemed to enjoy. When I groaned because I liked the salty taste of his pre-cum, he answered with a groan of his own. When I twisted my fingers around his shaft and swirled my tongue around the head of his penis, every muscle in his body tensed and he held his breath.

It was like having a salty Popsicle that never melted, attached to a lovely, sexy man who derived both pleasure and pain from my experimentation. It made me feel oddly powerful and light-headed. The skin was soft—impossibly soft—and so, so hot.

And quite abruptly it was over.

"Kaitlyn stop, stop…fuck, I'm going to come." He pushed me away, gripping himself.

My eyes widened at the sight of his big hand gripping his big dick. It was the absolute sexiest thing I'd ever seen. I wiped the back of my hand against my mouth, transfixed.

"Okay," I said, "tell me what to do. Should I lay down and you get on top?" Of course I was referring to the logistics of him releasing his semen on my breasts.

But it was too late. Martin gave himself two strokes and that was it. He spilled on his own stomach, angling himself down, his hand moving back and forth with jerky movements. I watched him as it happened. His body tense, his muscles cut in sharp relief, his face twisted for a very long moment in both agony and sweet relief, almost like he was confused and angry and listening to a choir of angels only he could hear.

Then he released a shuddering breath, brought his other hand to his face. He pressed the base of his palm against his forehead, like he was trying to keep his brain from exploding.

I smiled at him, waiting with anticipation for the post-BJ analysis. I found my shirt and wiped my hand dry, then placed it gently on his midsection; nevertheless, he flinched when the soft cotton connected with his still erect penis.

I cleared my throat, watched him absentmindedly clean himself, his breathing still labored. The pulse point on his neck pounded out a furious rhythm.

When he didn't move my smile waned. I was tired of waiting.

I poked him gently. "Martin…are you asleep?"

"No."

I waited for five seconds, then asked, "How was I? Did I suck?"

He laughed and it was mostly a good sound, velvety, seductive and satisfied; it wrapped soft tendrils of tenderness around my heart and squeezed, like a hug. It also rolled out the Slip 'n Slide in my pants and put up a sign that said *Ready for business time, only Martin need apply within.*

But it was also a smidge melancholy, and this smidge of melancholy made me feel nervous.

He sat up and swung his legs over the side of the bed, pausing only briefly before standing and walking to the bathroom. I watched him toss my shirt to the corner and leave, the sound of his laugh still vibrating in my ears and heart.

The water switched on and off. Martin returned almost immediately and reached for his discarded pajamas.

I considered him, then asked, "So, seriously, how did I do? Any pointers for next time?"

His movements faltered at this last question, then he finished pulling on his pants and said, "There won't be a next time."

His words were confusing and sad. He also looked a little sad.

"Why not?"

He ground his teeth and swallowed before answering, "I'm not doing this."

His words broke my heart, he sounded so raw.

"What?"

"This." He lifted his chin toward me.

"You have to be more specific."

"I'm crazy about you—"

"I'm crazy about you, too." I moved to stand, but his next words gave me pause.

"Stop!" He sliced his hand through the air, his voice harsh. He appeared to be struggling. "You know what I mean, Kaitlyn. I'm in love with you, and you're not...and I don't know why you did what you just did, but this is...this is so fucked up."

Martin pushed his fingers through his hair and turned away from me.

My heart took a kamikaze leap in his direction. "Martin—"

"No." He shook his head. I saw his eyes were closed, like he was trying to block me out, and I understood why he hated it when I closed my eyes or covered my face.

He continued, and I was relieved to see he did so with open eyes. "I don't want to be a pity project. And I don't want to push you into doing things you obviously aren't ready for."

"What makes you think I'm not ready?"

He faced me and gestured furiously to the bed. "Because you shouldn't be giving blow jobs to guys you aren't in love with. That's not who you are."

"What if I am that girl?"

"You're not! This, what we've been doing, every time I touch you, it means something to you more than just getting off. I can see it and I don't want that to change. I *need* it to mean something to you! I can't...I'm not doing this anymore."

"But what if I am in love with you?" I didn't think about the words before I said them. For better or worse, I just said what I felt at that moment.

He stiffened, winced.

"Don't..." I saw his eyes narrow, flash in the low cabin light. "Don't say it unless you mean it."

I stood from the bed and walked to him, driven by the momentum of our week together, our beautiful week. I felt that everything we'd done, all of our discussions and fighting and joking and challenging each other had led to right now.

My legs were unsteady, but I felt the crazy, nonsensical rightness of this moment in each of my nerve endings. I took his hand in mine and placed his palm on my left breast. My heart was beating sure and steady, but deep and hard—like my blood was viscous and my heart was working with effort. Then I covered his heart with my hand.

"I'm in love with you, Martin. And I'm saying it because I mean it," I whispered.

His gaze darted between mine and he blinked with hesitation, like I might disappear if he closed his eyes. Suddenly I was crushed to him, encircled in his strong arms, his mouth on mine, and he was walking me backward with stumbling steps to the bed.

"I want you," he said between kisses, my back hitting the mattress as he rose above me.

"I want you too," I said.

"God, I love you. I love you so much." He trailed a licking, biting, sucking path to the valley between my breasts, then back to my neck, frantic movements that told me he was overcome, wanting all of me at once. I was all waves and spikes of sensation, longing, and wound, taut desire.

"Say it again," he demanded.

"I love you," I breathed. And then again, this time for myself, because I felt it, "I love you."

He growled harshly, his hands tightening on my body in response.

"Please," he said, biting my neck, hot breath making me shiver, his hand at my breast, kneading. "Please, I need to be inside you."

I tilted my head back, offering him more of my neck. "I thought you didn't beg."

His hand skimmed from my breast to the waist of my shorts, sending a shock of goosebumps in its wake. His fingers pushed into my panties and between my legs, parting me, rubbing a tight circle over my clitoris, and making me cry out.

"I'm not begging," he said, entering me with his fingers. "I'm asking nicely."

I laughed, but then abruptly sucked in a sharp breath as Martin removed his fingers, grabbed my shorts, and pulled both my pajamas and my underwear down my legs. He took advantage of the moment to also shed his pants then reached over to the nightstand. When he returned I noticed a few things at once.

He was straddling me, his penis fully erect, entirely recovered, and jutting out from between his legs, not quite resting on my belly. The sliver of moonlight filtered through the underwater portholes, casting his beautiful body in blue-ish white relief. I reached for his sides, gripped him just above his narrow hips, loving the smooth texture of his skin over the hard planes of his muscles.

Glaring down at me, he brought a foil packet to his teeth and ripped it. My eyes widened at the sight because…sex.

We were going to have sex.

I was going to have sex.

In about two minutes or less I was no longer going to be a virgin.

Holy crap.

I wasn't sure what I thought was going to happen when I told him I loved him, and I wouldn't take it back because it was true, but immediate post *I love you* sex hadn't even entered my mind. According to Martin, one minute I wasn't ready to administer blow jobs, the next minute I was ready to lose my virginity.

"Whoa! Wait, wait a minute!" I held my hands up between us.

Martin didn't exactly wait, nor did he exactly move forward with the pending deflowering. Rather, his hands stilled right before he rolled the condom over his dick. Then he grabbed my wrists, held them down on the bed at my sides, and loved my breasts with his hot mouth and tongue and teeth.

"Tell me what you want," he said between inhibition-demolishing kisses, suckles, and bites. "Do you want me inside you?"

"Ah," I breathed as he released one of my wrists and brought his middle finger to my mouth; he dipped it inside. Instinctively I sucked on it, swirling it with my tongue. Then he trailed the wet tip from my chin, between my breasts, over my abdomen, and finally, *finally* parted my thighs and entered me. His middle finger stroked up and down, circling my center yet never quite touching where I needed.

"Because I want you, I want you so many ways." He bit the underside of my breast, making me jump. "Do you want me?"

I was going to say *yes*, but what came out instead was a breathy, "I'm on birth control."

He stilled. Groaned. His forehead dropped then pressed against my ribs.

"Fuck me," he said. Then I sensed him throw the condom to the floor. Sliding up my body to cup my cheek, his voice soft and serious as his eyes searched mine, "I'm clean, I promise. I would never take a chance with you."

I nodded and swallowed. I trusted him. I loved him. His body was heavy over mine and I felt less in control than I'd ever felt in my entire life. He must've read the fear in my face because he gave me a soft kiss then nuzzled my ear.

"You want me to eat your sweet pussy first? I'm going to taste you and make you come with my mouth. If you want more of me inside you, then you'll have to ask nicely."

My breathing was coming fast, pants of trepidation and anticipation. I had the fleeting thought that it hardly felt fair, leaving the entire decision to me when I wasn't the one who was experienced, when I could never be fully informed of what losing my virginity would feel like until after it happened.

He nipped my bottom lip then moved to explore his way down my body, but I caught his arms before he could go far.

His eyes came back to me and I knew mine were wide with alarm. "Wait…how bad is it going to hurt? On a scale from one to ten?"

He gave me a cherishing smirk and smoothed my hair away from my face, his eyes sobering, losing a bit of their haze of desire. "It doesn't feel great, Parker. There's a lot of bullshit out there. I've never heard of a girl getting off her first time."

"But you said you had, and I quote, '*fucked plenty of virgins…*' end quote. None of them have ever, you know, orgasmed? During their first time?"

Martin cleared his throat and glanced away, exhaling a little laugh. "You want to talk about other girls right now?"

"Yes and no. I don't need to know their names or what color their nail polish was or whether you loved any of them, but I'd like to hear at least some empirical data so I can make an informed decision."

"I didn't love them," he said suddenly. Frowning, he added, "But no, none of them orgasmed the first time."

"And other confounding variables?"

His frown softened. "Such as?"

"Were you wearing a condom?"

"Always."

"And did they love you?"

He hesitated. I could see he was thinking, and then answered with impressive honesty, "Yes. I think one of them did."

I bit my lip, my eyes blinking furiously. For some reason that thought made me feel numb.

He studied me, his fingers absentmindedly playing between my legs, like he couldn't help himself. I was alternating between aroused, very aroused, very scared, very concerned, and—finally—very aroused.

Then, on the vein of continuing his impressive honesty, he added, "I've never fucked anyone without using a condom. I've never thought about anything but protecting myself and getting off, and how good it feels while it's happening. It felt better if the girl is really into it, but it wasn't required. I've never…made love to anyone, and I've never been concerned about the girl's enjoyment more than mine. But, I swear to God, Kaitlyn," he licked his lips, his eyes darting between mine, "I want to make this amazing for you. I want you every day for the rest of my life. I don't want to hurt you, but I do want your body—just like I want your heart and your mind—and I do want to feel you lose control while I'm inside you."

I sighed, breathing out some of my fear and inhaling courage. I nodded, pressing my lips together. He kissed me, pressed the tip of his middle finger against my center, then whispered, "I'll make this so good for you, the next time you'll get on your knees and beg me for it."

I moaned, arching my back, which made him chuckle and place a wet kiss on my right breast.

"So beautiful," he said, trailing more slippery kisses against my skin, sending coiling heat to my core. "So fucking perfect." He bit my hip. It hurt, but it also felt wonderful.

He spread my legs wide, placing his large hands on the inside of my thighs and holding me open. He breathed on my center then licked me—hot and soft and slippery. He tongued my opening and slid the tips of his fingers along the inside of my thighs, tickling me and sending a new wave of shivering goosebumps racing over my skin.

He proceeded to tease me, his touches, lapping, licking, and stroking never enough to push me over the edge, but more than enough to drive me crazy.

I felt empty and needy.

So I reached for him, threaded my fingers through his hair to his temples, and said, "Please, please…"

Martin didn't ask for clarification.

He lifted to his knees, his rock-solid, imposing form rising above me. He wiped the back of his hand across his mouth. His eyes were hooded as they surveyed my open legs, my reaching hands, and my skin. I was bare to him. His right eyebrow quirked, just a little, and his smile was more sexy smirk than grin.

With measured, lithe movements, he stalked up my body, aligning himself at my entrance. I felt the swollen tip of him nudge me as he hovered above, watching me with avid, almost fascinated interest.

"Please, Martin," I moaned, my hands on his hips. My belly and pelvis felt aching and hollow. I angled my hips up, sliding against him.

I saw him shudder and heard him release a low growl. Then, seemingly out of patience, he lowered himself and kissed me—a soft, yielding, searching kiss—and a split second later, while his mouth was still loving mine, he pushed himself into me with one swift thrust.

I stiffened, a pinching, harsh, acute pain between my legs, and I whimpered.

"I love you," he whispered, his eyes holding my shocked, rounded gaze. He withdrew then pushed deeper.

I felt myself stretch. It was impossible and uncomfortable and I couldn't breathe. It hurt.

But each withdrawal was twice or three times as long in duration as his invasions and I was grateful. The slow, sliding movements brought me back to the pleasure he'd built with his mouth and hands.

Part of me just wanted it to be over, wanted to push him away, make it stop.

Yet his eyes, so cherishing and concerned, hopeful and reverent, grounded me. Then he dipped his head to my neck, releasing hot breath just under my ear, biting me and loving away the sting.

Whispered again, "I love you, Kaitlyn. I love you. You're perfect, and your body is perfect. I love you."

Finally, the inward strokes didn't hurt as much and, though I still felt uncomfortable, I didn't feel sharp pain.

With each careful rocking of his pelvis he placed a soft kiss on my face—my chin, my nose, my cheeks—the feather-light touches making me feel loved and utterly cherished.

I was nowhere near reaching my peak, but curiosity and some instinctual rhythm roused me from my paralysis and had me lifting my hips to meet his.

His hand pressed into my hip to still my movements.

"Kaitlyn, don't do that. If you…fuck, I'm going to…I can't…"

I spread my legs wider and flexed my inner muscles, enjoying the fiery—resentment? Warning? Desire?—in his eyes. I responded by narrowing my gaze and undulating my hips quicker, forcing him to match my rhythm.

"Stop, Parker, you have to... Oh God..."

Then his thrusts became inelegant and demanding. He became rigid. He grit his teeth and groaned.

And I watched all this, how he completely and totally lost control, with a roaring feminine satisfaction that was an excellent runner-up to an actual orgasm.

His body fell into mine like more than just gravity pulled him downward. He fit his hand between my back and the bed and embraced me, his breathing labored. I didn't mind the temporary, crushing weight of him or the slickness of his heated body. Being surrounded on every side by Martin was perhaps the best feeling of all time.

He lifted his head, his gaze searching and serious. He slipped one of his hands from beneath me, pushed his fingers through my hair and cupped my cheek.

"Are you okay?"

I nodded, giving myself a moment to be thoughtful about the matter, then said, "Yes. I'm just fine."

His gaze turned dark. "You're just fine?"

I nodded and patted him on the back. "You did good, Martin. It was painful. I'm not going to lie. But I'm not at all traumatized."

He stared at me for a beat, looking equal parts offended and amused. When he spoke, however, his tone was laced with demanding determination.

"We're not leaving this boat until you have multiple orgasms on my dick."

I felt my forehead wrinkle as my eyebrows pushed upward. "Multiple? Is that even possible? I'm pretty sure I read that was a myth."

"Parker..." He dipped his head to my neck, nibbled my earlobe, making me shrug my shoulder reflexively and shiver with delight.

He continued on a whisper, "If multiple orgasms are a myth, then you can call me Hercules."

125

[10]
MULTIPLE BONDS

THE SKY WAS overcast when Martin woke me up with kisses and bites on my shoulders. He insisted we go for a swim right then just in case it started to thunder or rain.

I later found this was also a slick kind of strategy because he jumped into the ocean naked.

I did not.

I dressed in the string bikini, daintily dipped my toes in, and then climbed down the ladder at the back of the boat. Martin eyed me over the gentle waves for about ten seconds while he treaded water. Then he lunged at me, chased me, caught me, easily discarded my bikini, and proceeded to feel me up.

We didn't make it as far as the bed. Instead, both of us feeling an irrational sense of urgency, we attacked each other in the water, then on the ladder leading to the deck, then on the deck. He pulled me down to his lap, straddling him, as he sat on the cushioned bench at the end of the stern. My breathing and movements were frantic, erratic, and when I came down on him we both cursed.

I'm not going to lie, it still hurt at first. But something about being naked under the sky, sticky and wet with sea water, learning each other, seeing the love and lust in his eyes, lubricated all the right spots. He guided my hips until I found a natural rhythm.

But I was distracted by the soreness between my legs and how my breasts bounced and swayed as I moved, until Martin leaned back on one elbow, his thumb moving to my apex, his eyes devouring me, and growled his appreciation. "This, you, here, now—hell, Kaitlyn. This is it, this is everything."

I did my best, but I wasn't proficient in the art of man-riding. I knew I was driving him crazy because he'd closed his eyes, obviously trying to hold off for as long as possible, his brow wrinkled into a severe frown of concentration which I would forever think of as the *don't come don't come oh God, don't come* face.

I'd been close for a while, but I was frustrated with my body's lack of accelerative progress. It was starting to feel nice, but I wasn't going to climax. Therefore I leaned forward and whispered, "Don't worry about me."

His eyes flew open and he stared at me with a ferocious kind of challenge. "What the hell does that mean?"

I lifted myself up then came back down, enjoying the sexiness of the act but somehow resigned that this time was going to be another miss.

He must've seen something in my eyes he didn't like, because before I could explain my meaning, he surprised me by standing, picking me up with him, and carrying me to the table.

"Lay down," he commanded.

I did.

He pulled out, spread my legs wide, knelt on the ground, and proceeded to have me for breakfast. It didn't take long before I was near spiraling, my lower belly tight with the promise of sweet, torturous relief. My hands gripping the edge of the table.

And I started chanting, "Oh God, oh God, oh God!"

And I came.

But then before I'd quite crested the wave, Martin stood and filled me, his thumb still circling my clitoris mercilessly in rhythm with his thrusts. And I came again—harder, better, faster, stronger—the rhythm of my blood thundering between my ears. The soreness between my legs adding a layer of exquisite pain to our combined pleasure...intensifying it. My mind was lost to everything except the sweet, overwhelming searing sensation.

I think I actually screamed, or yelled, or yodeled. I don't know what I did, but my throat hurt from the effort afterward. I hoped it wasn't a yodel...

He came a very short time later, looking overwrought, confused, and spent. Again he fell forward like a force other than gravity brought our bodies together. But this time he held himself up with bent arms and kissed my neck, chest, and shoulders hungrily.

My nerve endings felt fried so I let him play with my body, lick my skin, nip my nipples, and tongue my belly button as he slipped from me. His breathing returned to baseline after three or more minutes.

Then he said against my right ribs, "I love you. You're the most beautiful thing...so perfect."

I huffed a laugh, my hands reaching for, finding, then playing with the damp hair on his head. "I'm not perfect, but I'm glad you think so."

He brought himself back over me, so we were face to face, his gaze both curious and irritated. "Why do you do that? Why do you shrug off compliments? You are fucking goddamn gorgeous, Parker. You. Are. And you are a fucking goddamn musical prodigy. The fact you're not making music every day is criminal."

I gave him a sideways look and a small smile, wanting to choose my words carefully because he looked like he was considering some method of torture in order to push me into admitting my amazingness.

"I love that you think so, Martin."

"Kaitlyn—" His tone held more than an edge of warning.

"No, listen." I framed his face with my hands and lifted my head to rub my nose against his. I left a soft kiss on his lips and said, "I *am* glad you think I am all those things, and I believe you. But I'm not going to magically think I'm beautiful or perfect or talented just because you do. I have to get there for myself. I have to believe those things for myself—not because I have a boyfriend who values me and thinks I invented airplane neck pillows. If I base my self-worth on someone else's opinion or view of me, then I will also base my lack of worth on that person's opinion as well. And *that* has the potential of tearing me to pieces."

His eyes narrowed a fraction, but I saw reluctant understanding ignite behind his expression.

"Are you always like this?"

"Like what? Brilliant?" I teased.

"Yeah…brilliant."

* * *

I CAUGHT MARTIN staring at me no less than twenty times during the next few hours. And each time he looked a little dazed, like he was caught in the web of his own imagination. Sometimes I'd stare back, narrowing my eyes and administering a mock suspicious look. He'd smile—slow and lazy and sexy—then kiss me.

One thing was for certain: Martin Sandeke was using his big brain to work through an issue of enormous proportions.

Meanwhile, I worked on my last term paper in between conversations with Martin. He told me about his vision for the future of telecommunications and how satellites were going to play an essential role.

Science may not have been my passion, like I was wondering if music truly was, but I had a great deal of interest in science related topics. He told me all about the seventeen—SEVENTEEN!!—patents he held. Although, when I'd asked him if he was going to use the money from his inventions as the source for the sixty million he needed for the venture capitalist project, he'd laughed.

Inventing stuff, he explained, was fun. It was his hobby, but none of his inventions would ever bring in enough money.

When I asked him what he defined as enough money, he responded grimly, "Enough will be three times whatever my father is worth at any given time."

Seeing as how his father was a billionaire, this answer struck me as supercilious and off key. Making enough money sounded like an unhealthy obsession and dissonant with happiness.

I didn't voice this opinion.

By mid-afternoon the boat was ensconced in a torrential downpour, I'd grown used to his dazed stares, and—sadly—it was time to head back to the island.

We weren't going back to the big house, as we were going to the aforementioned cottage on the opposite side of the island, where Eric and Sam had been since Wednesday. I hoped she wasn't too irritated at me for my lack of communication...

I felt guilty about it, like a bad friend.

At present, Martin was in the captain's chair, steering us back, and I was trying to catch him unawares by lobbing rapid-fire questions at him, attempting to get him to admit something embarrassing.

"Favorite movie?"

"Wall Street."

"Favorite food?"

"Black licorice."

I paused, his answer surprising, but then pressed forward. "Favorite color?"

"Black."

"Black?"

"Yes."

I thought about this, then asked because I felt compelled, "How can it be black?"

"Most people's favorite color is black, but they're too fixated on what others think to admit the truth, even to themselves. Think about it, what color is represented in your closet more than any other? Is it blue? Green? Red? No. It's black."

"But black is depressing, it's the color of funerals and dark rooms and despair."

He gave me a half smile and almost rolled his eyes, but not quite. "In Japan, the color associated with funerals is white. Dark rooms can be fun. Also, black feels like something new to me, like the sky right before dawn."

"Martin Sandeke, that was almost poetic."

"You're easy to talk to." He didn't sound precisely happy about this.

"You say that like it's a bad thing."

"It might be. I say things to you I've never said or told anyone." He looked serious as he admitted this, gazing down at me with either resentment or longing, I couldn't tell which.

So I tried to disarm the sudden tension by saying, "That's because you *loooove* me."

He rolled his eyes. But he also smiled.

* * *

"SPILL IT."

"What?"

"*Everything.*" Sam elongated the word, over-pronouncing each syllable. "Spill it all. Spill it all over the place. Dump it out—on the floor, on the ceiling, on the duvet—spew it all, every last bit of it, because I am so far past interested, I've entered the neighboring territory of obsessively curious."

I glanced at her from the corner of my eye. She was staring at me, wide-eyed, mouth in a tight line, jaw set. It was her game face. She meant business.

It was nearly dinner time. We'd arrived about a half hour ago. Martin had anchored the boat and tied it to a small wooden dock adjacent to the cottage, then we'd raced through the rain to the cottage.

The cottage was actually everything I thought of when I thought *beach cottage*. It was cozy and small, had two bedrooms and one bathroom, a postage stamp kitchen with a breakfast bar, and a combined family room/living room. The place also decorated in nautical themes. Crafty mosaics of sea glass and shells lined the walls, and a big, rusty anchor hung above the front door.

Sam and I were currently in my room—well, the room Martin and I would share for the night—and I was going through my things. Sam and Eric had brought most of my stuff from the big house, but several items were missing; so far one of my textbooks, a folder of class notes, and several shirts. The textbook and the shirts were no big deal, but I needed the folder.

Also, it gave me an excellent excuse to postpone responding to Sam's questioning.

"Kaitlyn...you're stalling."

"I'm trying to figure out if all my stuff is here."

"You're stalling."

I huffed, turned to face her, and threw my hands in the air. "Yes. Yes I'm stalling."

"Why are you stalling?"

"Because I don't know how much I'm ready to share with you. I haven't decided."

"How much? How *much*?" she sputtered for a moment, her eyes sweeping up then down my body. "Well, how much happened?"

"A lot."

"Are..." Her eyes narrowed a bit as she considered her words. "Are you okay?"

"Yes."

"Are you and Martin okay?"

My serious face slipped as an involuntary and dreamy smile arrested my features. "Yes."

Her eyes went wide again. "Are you and Martin officially together? Like girlfriend, boyfriend, committed exclusive relationship, *I'll go bat-shit crazy and burn all your stuff if I find you with someone else* together?"

"Yes." I sighed as I said this, and it was a girly, wistful sigh.

However, Sam's expression was growing more anxious, pensive. "Did you...?" She licked her lips then nibbled on the bottom one, not finishing her question. Yet, the implied meaning was there. It hung over us both, the word *sex* in capital letters followed by a giant question mark.

I nodded, shifting my weight between my feet, unable to stand still.

"Oh my God." Her eyes lost a bit of their focus briefly and I couldn't tell what she was thinking. Then she blurted, "Please tell me he used a condom."

I felt a niggling bit of guilt or regret, which I pushed away immediately, instead deciding to roll my eyes. "Sam…"

"Kaitlyn, don't you *Sam* me. Please tell me you were safe."

"I'm on birth control," I whispered. I didn't know why I was whispering.

"So? Birth control doesn't stop genital warts."

"Sam…" Apparently my only defense against her commonsense facts was to roll my eyes.

"Kaitlyn, you are not stupid. So why are you acting stupid about this?"

"I trust him," I said without thinking, and shrugged.

Sam's eyes widened then closed, her chin dropped to her chest; I heard her exhale then say to the floor. "You think you love him."

I didn't respond. At my silence she lifted just her eyes. She looked sober, concerned, bracing.

I shrugged because, though I could guess the source and reasoning behind her anxiety on my behalf, I didn't share her worry. My feet were too far off the ground. I was basking in post-boat bliss. Martin loved me. I loved him. And the genital wart-covered world could go hide itself in a chemistry lab cabinet for all I cared.

"I do. I love him. I'm *in* love with him."

"Oh." She tried to smile, but it looked more like a grimace. "Well, that's…great."

I laughed at her effort to be supportive. "I know what you're going to say—"

Really, there were so many warnings she might give, concerns she might voice given the situation and how little she knew about Martin.

But instead she held up her hands to keep me from continuing. "I'm not going to say anything. Other than I hope you know that I will always be here for you should you ever need anything. Anything at all. *Anything.* And that includes a visit to the gynecologist or the name of a hit man."

I smiled at my friend because there was no doubt in my mind that she did love me. "You're a good friend."

She returned my smile, but worry still rimmed her eyes as she spoke, "You too, Kaitlyn... And you deserve the best, especially from Martin Sandeke."

Sam crossed the room and pulled me into a hug, and added in a whisper, "Never accept less than his best."

* * *

DINNER WASN'T UNCOMFORTABLE at all. It wasn't. Really, it wasn't.

Sure, Sam gave Martin the *I will cut you* glower at random intervals, but all in all, our foursome got along quite well. Her periodic awkward stare-downs were actually kind of funny because she'd typically pair them with ominous statements and dubious double entendre, like:

"Are you going to use the mustard, Martin? Or do you not use condom...mints?"

Then she'd lift her eyebrow meaningfully.

Another of my favorites was when we were discussing travel, places we'd like to go. Eric said he wanted to go to Australia and Sam blurted, "How about you Martin? Ever gone *Down Under*? Or is south of the equator not to your tastes?"

I noticed that Eric had to hide his smile and/or laughter behind his napkin on more than one occasion.

Martin didn't smile. Instead he'd answer her questions plainly, as though they were just normal questions; but I could see through his poker face that he thought she was equal parts funny and irritating.

After dinner and dishes were done, Martin pulled me away from Sam's suggestion that we play a game, setting his arm firmly around my waist.

"We're tired," he said.

"We are?" I glanced at him beseechingly, then back to where Sam was setting up Risk. Man...I loved board games. Especially games of world domination.

"We *are*." Martin narrowed his eyes at me and I wasn't so oblivious to realize he wanted more alone time.

I sighed my disappointment, then turned back to Sam. "I guess we're tired."

Her mouth was pinched and her eyes—appraising and unhappy—were moving between us, like she wanted to say something, but was quite literally biting her tongue.

I felt a small pang of guilt and mouthed, *I'm sorry*.

She gave me a small smile and shrugged as she packed up the game. "Don't worry about it. Maybe you can play another time…when *Martin* isn't so tired."

The pang of guilt blossomed into something else, something resembling unease. I didn't respond. Partly because I wasn't sure what to say, and partly because Martin was already leading me out of the room. But I finally found my voice when we made it back to our bedroom.

"Are you tired? Because I'm not actually tired. And, something you may not know about me, I really enjoy a wholesome game of vicious world domination every once in a while."

"I'm not tired." Martin pulled me into the room, shut the door, pushed me against it, and moved in for a kiss. His hands were already everywhere, like an octopus with opposable thumbs.

I turned my head at the last minute, bracing my hands against his chest. His lips landed awkwardly on my jaw, but he wasn't deterred by the misfire. Improvising, he kissed a wet path down my neck while his deft palms massaged my breasts through my bra.

"Hey, you." I tried to keep my tone light and conversational. "Maybe we could, um, slow down a minute and have a discussion regarding your feelings on world domination."

Martin's thumb swept over my nipple then he pinched me, hard. It felt good, sending spikes of Martin-juju-arousal-fog to the four corners of my body, but it also felt like a punishment, or retaliation.

"No," he said.

"No?"

"No."

The back of my head fell against the door and I huffed, liking everything he was doing, but disliking how single-minded he was being. In attempt to get his attention, I pinched the skin over his ribs.

"Ow!" He flinched a little, then laughed. It was a low, rumbly, sexy sound. Not at all the outcome I was going for. "Do you want to be rough?"

"No." I pushed *that* alluring thought away with all my willpower. "I want you to listen to me."

"And I want to bite you and lick you and fuck you and make you come."

"Ah, Martin—"

"Kaitlyn, stop talking." He moved his mouth to my ear and bit me before whispering, "I need to be inside you."

My body trembled with a little pleasure earthquake as his hands slid to the band of my shorts and down into my underwear, stroking me. I began to melt against him. My objections—and whether I actually had objections—grew muddled and distant. But then as he pushed inside me with two fingers I felt more than a twinge of soreness. I winced in response to the discomfort and I shoved at his chest.

"Wait. Stop, that hurts."

He stilled immediately, removing his fingers but not withdrawing his hand. Martin lifted his head and stared down at me, his green-blue eyes searching.

"That hurts?"

I nodded, swallowing before rushing to explain. "My pants aren't used to frequent invasions, or any invasions. It's been a busy week for my pants. As such, my pants need time to adjust, acclimate. My pants still like you a lot, but I think my pants need a rest."

He was so close, crowding me against the door. I could've counted his eyelashes.

"Your pants?"

I nodded.

"We're calling your pussy, 'pants'? That's what we're calling it?"

"No. I mean, we can...I guess. But 'pants' doesn't necessarily conjure the most alluring images. I'm open to other names if we have to name it. Why do we have to name it?"

His hand in my much-discussed pants slipped around to my bare bottom, caressing and squeezing. "We don't have to name it. I just thought you were naming it."

"No. I'm not naming it." I shook my head. "I was just saying, or trying to say, that the area in my pants that is required for sexual intercourse is—"

"You mean your pussy."

"Yes."

"Then say it. Say, *my pussy*."

I scrunched my face at him even as his hands continued to glide over my body and his hips rocked into me, making me feel muddled all over again.

"What? Why?"

"I just want to hear you say the word." Martin unclasped my bra.

"Why can't I say *vagina*?"

"No."

"Vag?" I tried, half serious.

He made a face then shook his head, pulling my shirt and bra from my body.

"How about my *nether region*?"

The side of his mouth quirked just before he took a step away to discard his own shirt, his fingers then moving to unbutton his jeans. "No."

"Dewy petals?" I batted my eyelashes at him.

"Ugh, what the fuck does that even mean?" He stepped out of his jeans, leaving his long, lithe, fine form in nothing but black boxers. He reached for me, and I let him.

"I have a ton of these." I grinned at his reaction. "I play this game, really it's a strange coping strategy, where I repeat synonyms for words—"

"I know. I told you, I heard you do it all the time during lab."

"Oh, that's right. Well, I know *lots* of euphemisms for the female anatomy."

"Don't tell me, I don't want to know." Martin turned us, marched me backward until my legs connected with the mattress, then eased us down using one arm wrapped around my middle and a single knee on the bed.

It was an impressive display of upper body strength and core muscles. In other words, it was hot.

"Just one more?"

His hand slid from my collarbone, between my breasts, and down my abdomen; he hitched two fingers into my shorts at my hip and paused.

"Okay, just one more."

"Meat curtains."

He frowned in a way that wasn't a frown, pressing his lips together valiantly before speaking mostly to himself. "This is what I get for falling in love with a girl who hides from me in lab cabinets instead of someone who wants to use me for my money."

Martin's eyes were bright with teasing, but they were also hot and focused. I could see his intentions before he licked his lips, his attention moving to my mouth.

So I blurted, "I need my vector calculus folder!"

"What..." He frowned at me, plainly confused, then asked, "Right now?"

"No. Not right now, but before we leave. I think I left it at the big house. I need it, as it has all my notes from this semester."

"Ah, well...I'll call tomorrow before we leave, see if Mrs. Greenstone can find it and bring it to us at the marina."

"Why don't we stop by on our way in the morning? I'm not one-hundred percent certain where it is."

"No. We aren't going back there." Ice entered his words; his declaration was almost hostile.

"But what if Mrs. Greenstone can't find it?"

"I'll call tonight. If she can't find it, I'll go over there by myself."

"That's silly. I'll be able to find it faster."

"If I can't find it then I guess I'll just have to tutor you in vector calculus."

I grimaced. "Seeing my own handwriting takes me back to the

moment when I took the notes and the lesson. It's the only way I can study. I have an unhealthy attachment to my class notes."

"Hopefully you also have an unhealthy attachment to me."

"So, how do you feel about me using you for your brain instead of your ties to massive wealth or the magnificence that is your body? I'd like to use it, often."

"What do you mean? Use what often?"

My back was resting on the bed now and he was over me, his bare chest against mine. I wasn't going to be able to think in this position, especially since I could feel his erection against my hip, so I smiled hopefully and pushed him until he was lying on the bed and I was hovering at his side.

"Listen, I don't want to mislead you. I *do* want to use you for your body, just so we're clear. But I'd also like for you to put that big head of yours to use."

He stared at me, and I realized too late that what I'd meant to say was brain...not head. Not. Head.

Martin fought a smile, and just looking at his handsome face made my stomach do a sudden backflip. He said smoothly, "Tell me more about what you'd like me to do with my big head."

I scowled at him. Surprisingly, I didn't feel a huge amount of embarrassment, just slightly flustered.

"Quit your backtalk or else I may have to pinch you again."

"I wouldn't mind, as long as I get to pinch you back." His hand moved to my breast and he fingered my nipple, making my breath catch and his already stiff erection tent his boxers.

"Stop it for a minute, I want to talk to you. I'm trying to be serious."

Martin's heated stare turned into a petulant glare and he removed his hands, sighed, and folded them behind his head. He blinked at me once, then moved his eyes to the ceiling. "Fine. What do you want to talk about?"

I didn't roll my eyes at his somewhat dramatic withdrawal, but I wanted to. Instead I pushed myself up and sat on the bed facing him, hugging my knees to my chest and started again.

"What I'm trying to say is that...I like *you*, Martin. I like your brain." I blurted the last part, not knowing exactly what I was about to say.

Just his eyes slid back to mine, the lines of his face thawing as he searched my face.

I tucked my hair behind my ears then rested my arms on the top of my knees, heartened by his open interest. "I like you. I like you for who you are, even though you're callous and don't quite know how to treat people. You're clever and funny. I admire the way you move and how you can't help but lead. I like how driven you are, and passionate. It's fun to watch. I also think there's a good heart in there, but I feel like it might be bruised and neglected..."

After I said the words I knew it was true. His heart was bruised and neglected. He needed mending, care, and comfort. He needed someone to trust.

I shook myself, realized I'd trailed off and we'd been sitting silently for a long moment, and turned my attention back to Martin. He was peering at me, waiting for me to continue.

I took a deep breath before speaking. "The thing is, I've been wanting to tell you this since Sunday. You have a friend in me. No matter what happens between us, I want you to know that if you ever need me—as a friend, as someone you can trust—I'll always be there for you. I'll always be your safe place."

Martin considered me for a moment, his gaze flickering over my face as though searching, before saying, "I don't think I'll ever want to be friends with you."

I must've made some outward expression that mirrored my inner surprised hurt because he gripped my leg to keep me in place and rushed to add, "I mean, I don't think I could ever be *just* friends with you. I could never be disinterested enough."

"Disinterested? You think friends are disinterested in each other?"

He half shrugged, his eyes moving to the right. "Yes. I have friends, but I'm not interested in them."

"Do you have any female friends?"

He nodded. "Yeah. My business partner is a woman. I'd consider her a friend and I couldn't care less who she's out with. But with you, I don't think I'd be able to see you with someone else and not go crazy."

"So, what? If we break up then you'll just cut me completely out?"

"I would." He nodded, looking very serious.

"Because you think you'll never be disinterested?"

"I know it."

"And by stating that you'll never be *disinterested* in me, you mean that you'll always want to…" I waved my hand in the air to finish my sentence.

His eyes moved back to mine and he grinned. "I'll always want to…?"

He was being obnoxiously obtuse, trying to force me to use his language.

"You'll always want to have intimate relations with me."

He shook his head like he thought I was cute, and clarified using his own vernacular, "Yeah, I'll always want to fuck you."

I scowled at him. "You know, it's one thing to use that word when we're," I waved my hand through the air again, "when we're in the middle of copulation. But it's completely different when we're sitting here and I'm trying to have a conversation with you about serious matters."

"Why? Why does it make any difference?"

"Because, it's crass and ungentlemanly."

"Ungentlemanly?" He looked like he was about to burst out laughing.

I increased the severity of my scowl. "Yes. Ungentlemanly. How you speak to me during everyday discussions matters because it's a direct reflection of how you see me and whether or not you respect me. Using bad language—yes, bad language. Don't give me that look."

He'd rolled his eyes and ground his jaw, like he thought I was being ridiculous. So I pointed my finger at him and wagged it.

"Using bad language tells me you don't have enough respect for me to use good manners or think about the implication of your words before you say them."

"Kaitlyn, you know I respect you."

"Yeah, you respect me so much you want to fuck me—not make love to me, not be intimate with me. Fuck me."

He grew still, the amusement and rebelliousness waning from his features, and he studied me. Though I got the impression he only half saw my face, and was mostly lost in his own thoughts.

At last he said, "I didn't mean it like that."

"But it's what you said."

His jaw ticked as he processed this information. A calculating gleam entered his eyes and they narrowed. "All right, how about this. I'll use more *gentlemanly* language during our everyday conversations if you use more *bad* language while we…during our periods of intimacy." He said this last bit in a flat tone, like he couldn't believe he was actually saying it in place of his favorite four-letter "F" word.

I considered his terms for less than five seconds. Really, there was nothing to consider. Using his bad language during lovemaking made sense…might even help me loosen up. Therefore I nodded and stuck my hand out for him to shake.

"Deal."

He smiled, fitting his hand in mine. "Parker, I love you."

"Sandeke, I see your love, and I raise you a secret handshake."

[11]

LINE SPECTRA AND THE BOHR MODEL

MARTIN RECEIVED A call in the morning that Mrs. Greenstone couldn't find my notebook.

Therefore, the next morning—after a forty-five minute argument, copious seething glares from Martin, and two hours of him giving me the silent treatment—we were all on our way to the big house to get my folder.

I couldn't take the chance he'd be unable to find it or abandon the search prematurely. I wasn't kidding when I told him I had an unhealthy attachment to my class notes. I was convinced the notes were the only reason I was getting As in all my upper-level courses.

Yes, my notes might have been somewhat of a security blanket for me, but so what? I needed them. I believed I needed them in order to succeed. I wasn't leaving the island without them.

We drove the rugged golf carts across the island, Martin and Eric in one, Sam and I in the other. The all-terrain vehicles were loaded up with our luggage and I was splitting my attention between Sam's chatter and her roll case threatening to fling itself off the cart with the slightest bump or provocation.

When we arrived at the mansion, Martin walked over and offered his hand to me. When I accepted it, he gripped mine tightly and studied my features; his were stormy and uncertain. When he made no move toward the house, I lifted my free hand and smoothed it over his cheek, lifted on my tiptoes, and brushed a soft kiss to his mouth.

"Hey, let's get this over with. We'll go in, get my folder, and get out. Maybe steal some cookies from the kitchen."

I watched him swallow. His features still stormy and undecided.

"If we run into my father, just do what I say. Just…" He sighed, closed his eyes, and ground his teeth. "This is a bad idea. You shouldn't be here."

I didn't know how to make this better for him, so I took three shuffling steps toward the house and tugged him after me. "Hurry up. I need those notes and we have a plane to catch."

He opened his eyes, giving me one last pained stare, then overtook my lead, pulling me after him. He paused just briefly with his hand on the door handle, as though mentally preparing himself, then opened the door quietly. We walked into the entrance and Martin searched the space briefly, loitering on the foyer steps. He seemed extremely reluctant to venture farther.

Before I could make an attempt to soothe his obvious tension, one of the most irritating sounds in the known universe halted our progress.

"Heya, Stroke."

Ack.

I knew that voice.

It was the cuss monster.

I looked to the left just as Martin did the same, then I glanced up at Martin's face. He was clearly perturbed and confused.

"What are you doing here? Why didn't you go back with everyone else?" Martin's grip on me tightened just a fraction as we turned to face Ben.

"Didn't see a good reason to go back yet," Ben said, before taking an obnoxious sip of what appeared to be a strawberry daiquiri through an oversized straw.

"Because I told you to leave. How about that for a good reason?" Martin's tone was flat, hard, and irritated.

I pressed my lips together to keep from making any kind of facial expression.

Meanwhile, Ben shrugged again, but sounded positively elated as he said, "But your dad invited me to stay, so I did. Besides, I've decided to quit the team, so you can go fuck yourself."

I felt tension roll through Martin—gathering—tangible in how he stood and the measured way he drew breath. But before he could respond, we were interrupted.

"Marty." This came from the top of the wide staircase and echoed through the foyer. The man waited until both Martin and I looked at him before continuing. His pale blue eyes rested on me. "I thought you'd left the island."

Denver Sandeke, Martin's father, was taller than I thought he'd be. Taller and not nearly as scrawny. He wasn't a good-looking man; his chin was almost non-existent and his nose was oddly shaped, thin and long. As well, he was either a member or the president of the hair club for men.

And with his entrance I felt a shift.

Whereas before Martin was and had always been the center of focus, the "alpha of the pack" as Sam put it, now his father's presence demanded the spotlight. In truth, neither of them clearly dominated the other. It wasn't shared power; it was dual power that co-existed very, very badly, like when two acid-base reactions are after the same proton.

"No," Martin said. The frost in the single word seemed to lower the temperature of the room by several degrees. It seemed that Denver, like his wife, brought out the Abominable Snowman in Martin.

Denver didn't respond to his son. Instead he sauntered down the steps, his eyes still on me, a friendly smile affixed to his lips. I noted that the shape of his mouth was similar to Martin's.

"You're Joss Parker's daughter." He sounded immensely pleased. Meanwhile something about the way he used my mother's first name made me want to pluck out all his nose hairs.

I started to respond, but Martin tugged on my hand and shifted so he was half blocking me from his father, like he was protecting me with his body. "We're leaving."

Denver ignored his son and offered me his hand. "It's so nice to meet you. I know your mother quite well. She is," he chuckled to himself, "she is certainly a force."

"Don't touch her." As Martin said this he moved me completely behind him, and with one hand on my hip, guided us a step back toward the door. I noted that he still faced his father, almost like he knew better than to turn his back.

My view of his father was obscured now that the mountain of Martin was between us, but I heard the change in Denver's voice as he addressed his son.

"You finally did something useful, Marty. You're still the village idiot, but at least your dick makes smart choices."

I heard Ben fake-suppress an obnoxious guffaw, but I barely registered it as my brain was still trying to grasp the venom that had erupted from Martin's father's mouth.

His father!

And yet, even knowing what I did about Martin, even knowing he had a history of callous indifference toward the feelings of others and had no qualms about yelling at men, women, children, and turtles, I was completely unprepared for his response.

"Better the village idiot than the village pervert and impotency expert. By the way, Ben here used your entire stash of Viagra earlier this week. You two flaccid assholes have so much in common."

Martin's father *tsked* and responded coolly, "Careful, Marty. Or I might decide to break your new toy."

"You even fucking look at her and they won't find your body." Martin took another step back, taking me with him.

This was completely crazy. I thought the run-in with his stepmother was vicious—this took vicious to a whole new level.

"You forget who bankrolls your life, *son.*" I winced as Denver said the word *son.* In context, coming from Denver's mouth, it sounded more like *whore.* "Your toys are my toys, and I'll use them whenever and however I please. Now step aside, you're not going anywhere until I say so."

I felt Martin tense. He released my hand and I saw both of his were balled into fists. He shifted on his feet, his stance bracing, like he was about to throw a punch. Martin was big, but his father was also big; as well, Ben the rapist was clearly on Team Evil's side. Two against one was hardly fair. I might be able to call for Eric before the situation escalated, but that was unlikely.

Tangentially, I wondered how many times Martin and his father had come to blows, but pushed the thought away for later contemplation. I couldn't stay where I was, silent, hiding. Now was not the time for me to hide, not when Martin was putting himself into harm's way on my behalf. I needed to *do* something.

Now was not the time to bow out gracefully. Now was the time to fight for Martin.

Since Martin was no longer holding me behind him, I stepped to his side and slipped my left arm around his right elbow.

Placing a thin smile on my face, I addressed Denver. "You'll forgive me if I don't shake your hand. As I've met your wife and see the company you keep," I nodded toward Ben, "you'll understand if I'm wary of communicable diseases. As Ben will tell you, not touching people I don't know is one of my life rules."

I was gratified to find my small speech had stunned all the testosterone in the room into inaction. Three sets of male eyes stared at me as though I were a strange creature.

I cleared my throat and continued, "I have no interest in knowing you, Mr. Sandeke. All I want is my vector calculus folder and then we'll be leaving."

Though Denver's eyes were on me, he spoke to his son. "I'm looking at her now, Marty. What are you going to do about it?"

Martin shifted restlessly at my side but I tightened my grip around his arm and responded for both of us, my voice conversational. "Again, I'll just take my vector calculus notebook and we'll be on our way."

"No. You won't." If Denver's wife had dead-face, Denver Sandeke had dead eyes.

Channeling my mother, I drew myself up straighter and glared at him square in his beady dead eyes. "Actually, we will. You see, Martin told me before we came over that you were a wee little worm of a man. Therefore, I made a call to my mother's security team. You may have heard of the US Secret Service? ...Yes? ...No?"

Mr. Sandeke shifted a half step back, his gaze narrowing on me.

"Ah. I see you've heard of them. Despite all their guns and shooting and whatnot, they're actually very nice men." I moved to side step him and pulled Martin with me, careful never to give him our backs. "Now, we'll just be getting that notebook then we'll get out of...well, we'll get out of your hairpiece."

* * *

On the up side, I had my folder. I also managed to collect my missing textbook and clothes—so, double bonus.

On the down side, Martin had barely spoken since we'd left the mansion. He also wouldn't look at me and had made no move to touch me beyond helping with my bags, offering me his hand on the boat, and guiding me to my seat on the plane—so, double whammy.

Also, his father was basically Satan, but with no chin.

Regardless, I didn't regret meeting the man. Meeting Denver swiftly explained many things about Martin, brought so much of his behavior and motivations into painfully sharp focus.

Now, as I eyeballed Martin from my seat, I noted that his face was red, flushed with color, and his eyes were a bit wild. I knew he was still thinking about his father and I knew his emotions were very, very near the surface. His seething anger radiated from him, like a billowing cloud of dark rage.

Honestly, I felt like one wrong move, or word, or glance, and he might trash the inside of the private jet...or scream at me. As such, all four of us had been silent. Even Sam saw fit to keep her sarcasm bottled up as she thumbed silently through a magazine like it held the answers to the perfect tennis game.

I was again faced with the reality that I didn't know the right thing to say to my boyfriend. As I stewed in this realization, I further recognized that being held hostage by his anger bothered me more than the possibility of getting yelled at.

My nagging disquiet grew as I watched him, his jaw clenching and unclenching, his breathing purposefully slow. He was so alone, entirely focused inward, lost in a dark place. This was where Martin Sandeke lived and how he'd learned to survive. I couldn't stand it.

I loved him.

Watching him fumbling through the labyrinth of his wrath was akin to my unreachable itch, except this time it was in my brain and heart.

Therefore, and acting completely on instinct, I unclicked my seatbelt, crossed to him, and sat on his lap. He stiffened, his razor eyes cutting to mine, laced with a fevered fury and severe warning. I ignored them.

Instead I encircled him with my arms, threading my fingers and nails into the hair at the nape of his neck, and whispered in his ear, "I love you, Martin. I love you."

He grew rigid for a split second, but then he embraced me. Really, he crushed me to him with his powerful arms and his forehead fell to my shoulder. We sat like that for several minutes—me gently scratching the back of his head and placing soft kisses everywhere I could, given my limited range of motion, and him holding onto me like a life raft. I silently rejoiced when I perceived the inflexibility wane, ease, relax, and his breathing grow normal, less measured.

He broke the silence with a growled, "I hate him."

"I can see why." I wanted to add that hating his father was counterproductive, as it gave his father all the power. But I didn't. I figured we'd have plenty of time in the future for me to help Martin deal with his poorly controlled rage where his father was concerned.

"He sent Patrice." He said this against my neck, his voice a broken whisper.

"On Wednesday morning? When I was in your room?"

"No. When I was fourteen. He sent her…to me."

My eyes narrowed with confusion and I stared at the side of his head. "I don't understand. What do you mean he sent her to you?"

I felt Martin gather a deep breath before he lifted his face from where it had been sheltered in my neck. He avoided my eyes, opting instead to stare at the cabin's ceiling and rest the back of his head against the headrest.

"After my mother died, I moved in with my father. I'd never...I'd never spent time with him before, but I'd always thought of him as a way to escape my mother's manipulations. During the first year he ignored me. Then something changed when I was fourteen. Everything was a test, all of our interactions were mind-games and I was always failing, and he always let me know how much of a disappointment I was. I wanted to prove myself to him. I thought I could earn his respect."

Martin's eyes darted to mine and he gave me a wan smile shaded with bitterness as he continued. "I was so fucking stupid, naïve. I thought no one could be worse than my mother, and I'd worshiped my father. But I was wrong."

I studied him, thought about what it must have been like for him as a shy, beautiful boy to be at the whim of a fame-seeking mother, then thrust upon his unfeeling, manipulative father. I'd been allowed to hide in closets. He had not. My heart broke for him.

As well, his earlier statement, about his father *sending* Patrice to him nagged at me, filled my stomach with dread.

I prompted gently, "What did you mean, your father sent Patrice to you when you were fourteen?"

He heaved a sigh. "When I was fourteen she climbed into my bed. She was naked. I was asleep. She put my hands on her body and kissed me, touched me..." He said this like the words were sour and swallowed. "I woke up and realized what was happening, so I pushed her out of the bed and my room. The next morning I went to my father and told him what happened—this was before they were married, so I figured he'd leave her. Instead he laughed at me. He told me he'd sent her, that it was a test, and that I'd *finally* passed a test."

"Test? What kind of test?"

Martin held my gaze as he explained, his tone hollow. "He had to marry her, she has something incriminating on him, but I'm not sure what. But he wanted to keep his money out of her reach, so it was a loyalty test. I think he liked the irony of using her to ensure her undoing. Shortly after that he transferred all his property into my name using a trust."

"What about his bank accounts? Surely she can just raid those in a divorce?"

He shook his head, adding impassively, "No. In their state of residence, draft accounts existing prior to marriage, even new deposits, aren't community property, nor are retirement, stock options, and savings. That's why the houses—the ones he owned and the new ones he's purchased—are in my name. They're in a trust until I turn twenty-one."

"So...next year?"

"No. Four months."

I stared at him, nonplussed. I'm sure my eyebrows were drawn together in a severe frown of equal parts anger and disbelief. I shook my head at this elaborate scheming, the disgusting test of loyalty that had obviously humiliated and scarred Martin, and felt the acidity of furious indignation rise in my throat, building a concrete structure in my chest.

But before I could vocalize my horrified amazement, Martin added in a voice so quiet I could barely make out his words, "Then he told her. He told Patrice she could use me if she wanted."

"He what?!" I blurted. Actually, it was more like a shriek.

"She didn't—she tried, but she didn't get a chance. I wasn't at the house much after that."

I was so angry. My eyes were burning and fury choked my throat. Therefore, without meaning to, I expelled my acrid thoughts. "What a goddamn, motherfucking sonofabitch."

He laughed a little, obviously surprised, and his answering smile was small and sad. "I don't know. I never met my grandmother."

I huffed a laugh, but my features twisted with sadness and anger, and I wanted to make everything better for him. Yet I felt completely helpless. I noted he was avoiding my eyes again; as well, his earlier rage had dissipated and seemed to be replaced with a simmering and fierce determination.

I moved my hands to frame his face and feathered a soft kiss over his lips. "I wish I could drop a house on your father," I whispered.

His mouth tugged to the side, so I kissed the side of his mouth.

"No...I'll make sure he gets what he deserves."

I lifted an eyebrow at this statement and leaned back just far enough so I could look in Martin's eyes. "What he deserves is your apathy."

His eyes flashed and I felt his fingers flex on my body as he contradicted through clenched teeth. "No. What he deserves is to be ruined and humiliated."

My gaze moved over Martin's features and I saw passion there. It was dark passion, potent and fathomless. I was certain he was absolutely intent on being the instrument of his father's destruction.

It hadn't occurred to me until that moment that he might not want to work through the issues with his father. Rather, it appeared his zealous loathing for his father might currently be the driving force in his life.

"Martin—" I started, but stopped, unsure how to proceed but needing to say something. I swallowed as I searched his eyes for some thread of sanity and reason where Denver Sandeke was concerned. I found none. "Martin, maybe take a step back from this. I understand your father is a horrible man who has done horrible things, but what can be done? He's very powerful."

"He's not untouchable," he was quick to point out, his eyes growing a darker shade of blue as he added, "and I have a plan..."

"But why waste your energy on him? Why not forget him, cut him out of your life like the cancer he is, and move forward with your—"

He shook his head while I spoke, his jaw tight with steely determination, and interrupted me. "No. Fuck no!"

I flinched and his grip tightened on my body as he continued with a harsh whisper, "Nothing else matters other than making him suffer. *I'm* going to be the one to destroy him. Seeing him humiliated is all I've thought about and planned for since I was fourteen. If I achieve nothing else in life, if I do nothing else…" He ended there, his eyes losing focus as his thoughts turned inward to a dark place I couldn't follow.

My disquiet spread, trepidation ballooning with the dawning comprehension that Martin had allowed this passion—this hatred for his father—to define him.

And most of all, more than the tragic and twisted tales of his childhood, this realization broke my heart.

[12]

FACTORS AFFECTING SOLUBILITY

T HE PLANE LANDED and I was in a mood. An introspective, anxious, overthinking-the-situation mood.

Whereas Martin's mood had lightened considerably.

When we stepped off the plane and piled into the limo, my mood did not improve. Eric and Martin discussed what to do about Ben's abdication from the team. Sam tossed me searching looks. I stared out the window.

When we arrived at the dorm and the boys carried our luggage into the building, my mood did not improve, not even when Martin pulled me into an abandoned study room on the first floor and motioned for Sam and Eric to go on ahead. Not even when he backed me up against the door, crowded my space, his eyes dark and hot with intent.

Not until he said, "I told you because I trust you, Kaitlyn. I don't want anything—least of all my fucked-up past—coming between us."

I held his gaze and felt some of the tension ease from my shoulders, leaving me feeling merely melancholy. "Thank you for trusting me. I'm just...I'm just so sorry you had to go through that. I know trusting can't be easy for you."

"You make it easy." His eyes lit as he caught my wrists, and used his body to press me against the door. Martin's voice dropped an octave as he added, "Being with you, listening to you play music, calling you on your bullshit…"

I lifted an eyebrow at this, feeling acutely peeved and opening my mouth to protest. He grinned and spoke faster to keep me from interrupting. "…touching you, kissing you, watching you come, making love to you…you make everything right."

I felt my cheeks warm as he held my gaze and his lips slowly descended to mine. I lifted my chin to meet his mouth, anticipating his kiss, hungry for it.

Martin released my wrists as his mouth slid over mine, his greedy hands moving under my shirt to the bare skin of my torso. When we parted, my fingers were twisted in his hair and I was breathless; as well, he'd built a fire in the vicinity of my pants.

He was basically an Eagle Scout of pants fires.

So I groaned and pleaded, sounding silly and pathetic to my own ears, "I miss you already. Will you stay? I could spend some time calling you on *your* bullshit, or we could study chemistry."

"Or make out."

"Isn't that what I just said?"

He laughed, stole a fast kiss, and then hugged me to him. I returned his embrace and felt him speak against my hair. "I have to go back to the house, make a few calls, take care of some business. But then I'll come back and stay as long as you want me to stay."

I nodded, nuzzling his chest, and smiled, thinking how intoxicatingly wonderful it was to have the promise of an evening with Martin in my immediate future.

* * *

I was in a much better mood when we walked into the suite area of my dorm room, and right into the tall, straight, hard chest of a secret service agent.

No one ever expects the secret service.

I backed up, excusing myself, and stepped on Martin's foot as he was following close behind me. He held my shoulder with one hand, and shifted us both away from the agent. My mind went around the Ferris wheel of confusion only twice before I realized that the presence of the secret service could only mean that my mother was someplace nearby.

I was expecting her for brunch on Sunday, as per our earlier discussion.

Her plans must've changed.

"Oh, hello," I said automatically, reaching out my hand to the man, "I'm Kaitlyn Parker."

The man was dressed in a black suit, black tie, and white shirt; his sunglasses were tucked in his coat pocket and I caught my reflection in half of the lens peeking out of its home.

"I'm Stevens." Stevens accepted my hand for an efficient shake, his dark brown eyes skating over Martin then back to me. His tone was equally efficient. "Ms. Parker, the senator is waiting for you in your room."

"Okay." I nodded and glanced at Martin over my shoulder as I searched for the handle of my suitcase behind me. "Hey, you want to meet my mom?"

His eyebrows jumped and he shifted on his feet, relinquishing the luggage to my care. "Uh…sssssure."

It was easy to see he was caught by surprise, so I waited for a beat, turned, and studied his face. "You don't have to. You can go make your calls and come back later. There is no pressure here. She can be kind of intimidating."

He gave me a bantam smile, really just a hint of one whispering over his lips, and his tone turned teasing. "Really? Intimidating? I hadn't heard that about your mother…who is a *US senator*."

I narrowed my eyes at him and pressed my mouth into a flat line to keep from laughing; I turned back to the agent and asked, "Do you need to frisk him? I can do it for you if you want."

Martin made a choking sound behind me.

The agent did not smile. "Yes, ma'am. I will need to search him before he approaches the senator."

I nodded and walked around the secret service agent, then turned and walked backward toward my dorm room door.

"See you inside," I said cheerfully. I also winked at him.

He scowled at me, but then had to move his attention to the agent who was instructing him to put his hands out, palms up.

I snickered and walked into my room. I found my mom sitting in the chair next to my microwave talking on her cell phone. She was dressed in her typical outfit: an expensive, nicely tailored pantsuit accessorized simply with an American flag lapel pin. The cut and style remained constant, but the color varied between blues, black, and greys. Today she was in black.

Her eyes lifted to mine as I entered and she smiled warmly, pointing to her phone then lifting her index finger in the universal sign for, *give me one minute.*

I nodded and placed my suitcase on my bed, returning her smile. I unzipped the bag and began emptying its contents to keep myself busy...because I found I was equal parts nervous and excited. I really, really wanted her to like Martin—so, nervous. And I was certain she would like him—so, excited.

Everything with Martin had happened so fast; in some ways I was still on that speeding train, because it didn't occur to me that my mother meeting Martin would yield anything but stellar results.

Turns out, she really did only need a minute to end her call. In fact, I think she clicked off without saying goodbye.

As she stood and pulled me into a quick hug, she said, "I hope you don't mind, I asked Sam and her friend if we could have the room for a few minutes. She dropped her things off just a moment ago."

I shrugged and returned her fast embrace. "No, no. That's fine. I think she has to go check in with her tennis coach anyway."

She released me and folded her hands in front of her. She never crossed her arms. When she stood still she always folded her hands. She told me once that early in her career folding her hands kept her from fidgeting. Now she did it out of habit.

"Good. You must be wondering why I'm here a day early and without your father." Her gray gaze moved over me searchingly, like she was cataloguing changes in my appearance.

"I told George I wouldn't be back until today when I called him last week. I hope you got the message."

"Yes. Your unexpected trip. That's partially why I'm here." My mother's eyes finally settled on mine and I detected a slight hesitation in her usually confident voice.

I frowned, casting her a sideways glance. "Is everything all right?"

Her eyes softened in an alarming way, and she opened her mouth to respond. But then she quickly snapped it shut and glanced at the door over my shoulder. I followed her gaze and found Martin hovering at the entrance to my room. I couldn't help my giant smile.

"Oh!" I reached for his hand, not really registering the stoic mask that had slipped over his features as I tugged him into the room and turned back to my mother. "Mom, this is Martin Sandeke. Martin, this is my mom, Joss Parker."

I knew I sounded positively giddy as I made the introductions, but I couldn't help it. I was so excited. I loved my mother, and was so proud of her. She was my superhero. I was her biggest fan.

And now I was introducing my Martin to her, this boy I loved so much.

I figured that since they were both amazing and brilliant, and had wonderful thoughts about the future of Big Telecom and technology, the two of them would immediately fall into a stimulating conversation on the subject. I ignored the fact that Martin's intentions weren't entirely altruistic because the outcome of his plans would benefit society just the same.

I glanced between them as they shook hands, grinning, waiting for the stimulating conversation to begin.

It didn't begin.

Instead I watched as my mother became Senator Parker, her gray eyes adopting their steely and coldly assessing glint as she looked Martin up and down.

"Senator Parker," he said.

"Mr. Sandeke," she said.

My stomach sank at their mirrored frowns and frosty posturing. I winced and tried to swallow, a thick, foggy numbness unfurling in my stomach as comprehension struggled to dawn and silence stretched.

No one said anything for a full minute. Actually, no one said anything *verbally* for a full minute. Instead they stared at each other and a form of silent communication passed between them. My heart thumped uncomfortably as I struggled to find words to make everything better, explain that Martin was a good guy, that he wasn't his father.

But just as I opened my mouth to voice this as fact, Martin bent, gave me a soft kiss on my cheek, and whispered in my ear, "I'll see you tonight."

He gave me a tight, apologetic smile that didn't reach his eyes. He turned away. He left.

I stared after him, blinking at the door, wondering how everything could have gone horribly wrong in one and a half minutes when absolutely nothing had been said.

My mother's soft sigh pulled my attention back to her and I struggled to speak. Finally I blurted, "He's wonderful. He's really wonderful. He hates his father, and you're going to love him. He has ideas about satellites and he invented lazy fishing poles...and I don't understand what just happened."

She gave me a sad smile—hers didn't reach her eyes either—as she crossed the three steps to the door and shut it; she turned back to me and folded her hands.

"Kaitlyn, Martin Sandeke is why I am here, one day early, and without your father."

I frowned at her, searching her face for a clue but found only patient concern; at a loss, I vocalized my confusion. "I don't understand."

She sighed again. She hardly ever sighed. I felt a nagging sense of disquiet.

My mom placed a hand on my shoulder and guided us both to the bed until we were sitting, facing each other; then she said in her normal, businesslike tone, "My office received a call from a reporter at the Washington Post yesterday asking me to comment on my conflict of interest regarding the affordable telecom bill. He questioned my ethics if I remained in the chair position on the Commerce, Science, and Transportation committee because my daughter is in a serious relationship with the son of this country's largest telecom provider's CEO."

"Wait…what?"

"It seems he has pictures of you and Martin during your vacation and sound bites from one of your fellow students, a Mr. Benjamin Salsmar, who was with you this last week, indicating that the two of you are very serious, and that our families are quite close."

Benjamin Salsmar. Benjamin. Ben. Ben the bottom-feeding rapist, cuss monster!

UGH!

"Ugh." I shook my head as my face fell into my hands. "*That's* why Ben was still there this morning…what an asshole."

I heard my mother clear her throat. I hadn't thought before I spoke; I was pretty sure this was the first time she'd ever heard me cuss. To her credit, she made no comment about it, even though she'd told me when I was younger that curse words weren't adult language and had been mischaracterized as such.

She'd once explained that curse words were used by the idiots, and unimaginative members of our society, individuals who never learned actual adult language—i.e. multisyllabic descriptive words—and flung curses around during childish temper tantrums.

Nevertheless, Ben *was* an asshole.

But aside from Ben's assholery, what he'd said—what he'd told the Washington Post—was fifty-one percent true. Martin and I were in a relationship. I was not ashamed of it or of him, but I was now beginning to see that our relationship might cause some professional problems for my mother.

After several seconds she asked softly, "What is going on with you and Martin Sandeke?"

I gathered a calming breath and straightened, letting my hands drop from my face. I met her eyes and told her the truth. "Martin and I are dating."

"I see..." Her thoughtful expression didn't change except that her eyes narrowed just slightly. After a short pause she asked, "How long has this been going on?"

"About a week."

"Oh. Then it's not serious."

"No. It is serious."

"After a week?"

"Yes," I responded firmly.

She inspected me for a long moment, her gaze searching and tinged with slight confusion, but then she conceded with a nod. "Okay. If you say it's serious, then it's serious."

I stared at her. She stared at me. I waited for her to say something, to give me the right answer.

When she didn't, I blurted, "Mom, I can't just walk away from Martin. I think I'm...I mean, I've fallen in love with him. We're in love with each other. I love him."

My mother's face softened at this news, but her eyes held pity and worry. "Oh, Kaitlyn." She placed her hand on my shoulder and squeezed, her gaze moving over my face. "Honey, from what I know about Martin Sandeke, he's not the kind of boy who is going to be gentle with your heart or appears to do anything without an ulterior motive. As such, I find this news worrisome."

I tried to give her my best responsible young adult face. "Yes. I can guess what you've discovered about him. But I've spent a week with him—with just him for the most part—and he is not who he appears to be. He is...he is amazing and so kind."

"He's kind?" Her tone held a note of disbelief.

"He's kind with me."

"But not with everyone." This wasn't a question. It was a statement of fact.

"No, not with everyone. But if you knew—"

"And you've fallen in love with a person who doesn't feel it's necessary to be kind to anyone else but you?"

I pressed my lips together and swallowed. She didn't sound judgmental or even upset. She sounded curious. It was always this way with my mother. Her curiosity was why she won every argument, and why people always listened to her and took her advice.

She was exceedingly reasonable. She was never malicious or pushy, never condescending or irritated. She was only curious. She'd poke holes in terrible proposals and theories with her curious questions until it was clear to everyone that the proposal or theory was garbage. But she'd never, ever come out and say it.

I'd learned that the best defense against curiosity is honesty.

"Yes. I'm in love with a person who doesn't feel like it's necessary to be kind to anyone else but me."

"I see." She nodded thoughtfully, her eyes narrowing as she examined me. I could see her brain working, considering all the data, working through the scenarios.

I prepared myself for a detailed curious onslaught. Instead, she surprised me.

"Kaitlyn, I trust you. You know what's at stake." Her tone was firm, almost hard. "I've explained the situation and you are exceedingly bright. You understand the ramifications of staying in a relationship with Martin—and not only to my career and me, which is really the secondary issue here. The primary issue is what this does to the American public. You understand that Martin's father is using this relationship to expel me from the chair position of the Commerce, Science, and Transportation committee. He will succeed because he is right."

"But…but how is he right? How can he do that?"

"He is right because I will have an intrinsic bias if my daughter is in a serious relationship with this country's largest telecom provider's Chairman of the Board and CEO's son. That is a fact. I will resign before I am forced out, because perception of bias is just as damaging as actual bias. Mr. Sandeke has been positioning Senator Neimann to take my position for the last two years, both with the Vice President and the President pro tempore of the senate. He is the handpicked replacement and he will kill or bury the affordable telecom act—you know this is how Washington works—and those Americans in rural areas will continue to be unable to access affordable high speed services, thereby placing them at a prolonged disadvantage over those living in urban city centers."

I blinked at her, at all her facts, and ground my teeth. "So I can break up with Martin until the bill passes or stay with him and ruin the lives of millions of people?"

Her expression turned sad. She took a deep breath like she wanted to say something but hesitated, thought better of it.

"What? What do you want to say? Just say it."

She sighed. Again! And her next words surprised me because they sounded shockingly maternal. "You know I trust your judgment, Kaitlyn. But...I'm worried about you. I wonder, have you considered the possibility that perhaps Martin's feelings for you are not what they seem?"

I stiffened, leaned slightly away from her. "What is that supposed to mean?"

She pursed her lips, and her eyes darted to the door then back to mine. "Martin's father is a very intelligent man, and he's equally calculating. He has acuity for industrial strategy like I've never seen. As well, he's known to use those closest to him as part of his strategy. Seven years ago his wife—yes, his current wife—was at the center of a sex tape scandal with Senator Peterson from Wisconsin. You likely don't remember because you were only twelve or thirteen."

She paused and I noted she looked extremely uncomfortable. She took a deep breath, and her eyes searched mine. "Senator Peterson was the chair of the Commerce, Science, and Transportation committee at the time, the position I hold now. This bill that Martin's father has been fighting so hard to bury is a reimagining of Senator Peterson's bill from seven years ago, before an ethics panel removed Peterson from the position during the investigation."

I frowned at this news and the obvious conclusion I was supposed to make. "That's not what's going on here. Martin isn't dating me because his father told him to."

"Are you sure?" she pressed. "Because I've been under constant scrutiny from the ethics board since I took this chair position. Your father and I have been audited three times by the IRS. Denver Sandeke and his lobbyists have been relentless. The last time I saw him he actually suggested we open negotiations for affordable service. I was stunned and I took that as a victory—because he's never given an inch before last month. I assumed it was because he's been unable to discredit me…but now I'm wondering if this trip you've just taken with Martin was part of his plan."

I stared at my mother, my stomach made queasy and sick by her suggestion. "You think it's so impossible Martin would just be interested in me for me?"

Her eyes widened, then her entire stance changed. She looked horrified. My mother grabbed my shoulders and turned me so we were facing each other directly. "God, Kaitlyn…no. No. Absolutely not. You are a treasure, and I'm not saying this just because I'm your mother and I'm proud of you. I'm saying this because it is the truth. It is very likely that these two issues—Martin's feelings for you and his father's manipulations—have nothing to do with each other. But I needed to ask the question. Based on historical data, how Mr. Sandeke has conducted himself in the past, the question had to be asked. You understand that, right?"

I nodded, believing her, but saying nothing.

She sighed again and I could feel her frustration with the situation. Actually, she looked frazzled. I'd never seen her so discomposed and my stomach soured further because *I* was the cause of her worry. I felt like a disappointment.

"Kaitlyn, we can only try to do our best. I am trying to do my best here. The situation is impossible for me to solve, and that's why I'm leaving it in your hands. You have all the facts. There will be hundreds of bills, and there is always good work that needs to be done. If I resign from the committee and this bill fails, then I will refocus my energy on something else. But," she paused to make sure I was looking at her as she finished, "I have only one daughter."

I pressed my lips together, feeling miserable and conflicted.

My mother must've seen my struggle because she lifted her hand and cupped my cheek in an uncharacteristic display of affection. Her eyes were reassuring, yet resigned. "I'm not going to insist on making this decision for you. You have to decide what's wrong and what's right for yourself."

[13]

VAPOR PRESSURE AND BOILING POINT

AFTER MY MOTHER left, leaving the crushing weight of this decision in my hands, I spent the next hour fretting and chasing circular logic in my head. I had no right answer, but I recognized I had two options.

I could hide in the closet and wait for everything to resolve itself.

Or I could talk to Martin, lay it all out there, and insist we work together to solve this conundrum.

In the end, I realized I couldn't go back to being the closet girl. Over the past week something within me had fundamentally shifted. I would never be content as a closet-dweller again. I was out of the closet...in a manner of speaking.

So, really, I had one option.

Once I decided Martin and I would work through this together, I absolutely could not wait to discuss the matter with him. Therefore I grabbed my jacket, ran down the three flights of dorm stairs, and jogged to Martin's fraternity house.

I was still very much in my own head when I spotted Griffin on the front porch, carrying a ladder to where three other guys waited with nails and a sign. Paying the other three no notice, I jogged straight to Griffin.

"Hey, Griffin."

"Kaitlyn, hey. Are you here to see Martin?" He handed the ladder off to one of the three and gave me a warm smile.

"Yes. That's why I'm here. Can you take me to him?"

"Yeah, yeah. Sure." He didn't hesitate. He turned for the door to the house and assumed I'd follow. I did.

We climbed two sets of stairs and navigated through a tangle of hallways, all with dark wood floors and beige paint. No art donned the walls; I tried to make a mental topographic map just in case I arrived to visit Martin in the future but encountered no friendly tour guide.

At last Griffin stopped at one of the doors—much like any of the others—and knocked three times.

"Hey, it's Griffin—"

"Go away."

"—and I've got Kaitlyn with me."

Griffin gave me a small grin and a quick wink when the last part of his announcement was met with silence followed by approaching footsteps.

The door swung open, revealing a shirtless, sweaty Martin Sandeke. He was dressed only in shorts, socks, and shoes, and he'd obviously just returned from a run. Martin's eyes landed on mine immediately and he appeared very pleased to see me. I was very happy to see him, sweat and all.

Actually, his chest was so perfect it glistened.

I had a boyfriend that glistened, and not in a weird shimmering kind of way. In a manly, super sexy, flawless kind of way.

Oh...sigh.

I smiled at him, because that's what one does when faced with a glistening, shirtless Martin. You just do it. It's a law of nature, like gravity or eating cookies when they're hot out of the oven. No. Choice.

I was about to say hi, but he cut me off by reaching forward, grabbing my hand, pulling me into his room, and shutting the door.

I was about to say hi again, but I was cut off by the sound of Griffin's muffled voice from the hallway. "Okay then, you're welcome. I guess I'll just get back to what I was doing."

"You do that," Martin responded absentmindedly, his gaze moving over my face like he hadn't seen me in days instead of hours.

Finally, hearing Griffin's retreating steps, I laughed lightly and was just about to say hi again, when Martin kissed me. He braced his hands on the door at my back and devoured my mouth. I lifted on my tiptoes and tilted my chin to provide better access, but when I reached for his body he pulled away.

"Don't." He stopped the progress of my hands by holding them between us. "I need a shower. I just got back from a run."

"I don't care." I shrugged, knowing my traveling stare was some-what hazy and a lot greedy as I scanned his torso; and then, because I finally could, I said, "By the way, hi."

At my good-natured greeting, I saw his shoulders visibly relax and he returned my smile. "Hi."

"It's good to see you." I exhaled, feeling better about…everything now we were face to face. My back was to the door and he was standing in front of me, holding my hands in both of his.

"It's good to see you, too." His tone was relieved, sincere; but I noted he appeared to be somewhat cagey, bracing. "How was the visit with your mother?"

I closed my eyes briefly and shook my head, opening them again before responding. "It was…troubling."

He released my hands and crossed his arms over his chest. "I don't think she likes me."

"When she gets to know you, she will like you."

Martin's smile was crooked and my allusion to the future seemed to comfort him. He nodded, like he believed me. "Yeah, eventually she'll come around."

"Yes. Eventually. I'll just have to bring you home with me over summer vacation. You and my dad can talk nerd stuff."

"You talk nerd stuff, too." Martin turned and crossed to his dresser.

"Well, then all three of us will talk nerd stuff at the same time. It'll be a nerdy conversation trifecta." I took three steps into his room and surveyed the space. It reminded me a lot of the room back at the island where he slept: small, cluttered with personal things, small twin bed, comfy comforter and pillows. I liked the absence of sterile and fancy appurtenances.

He was rummaging through his drawers, obviously looking for something in particular, when he called over his shoulder, "So, you said her visit was troubling? What happened?"

"Oh, ugh!" I rolled my eyes, remembering the purpose of my visit was unfortunately *not* to ogle Martin's glistening chest of perfection. Flopping on his bed I didn't try to disguise my aggravation with the subject. "That's actually why I'm here now instead of waiting for you tonight. I need your help."

He stopped his search and turned toward me, his forehead marred with obvious concern. "What can I do?"

"Well, it's...the whole thing is completely bizarre. But I think we can figure this out together."

"Parker, what's going on?"

I heaved a big sigh, gave him a small smile, then proceeded to detail the gist of the conversation I had with my mother. When I got to the Ben part, his eyes narrowed and he ground his teeth. He looked irritated, but not exactly surprised.

"He's always been a fuckwad," Martin ground out, slamming his dresser drawer shut.

"Yes, well...rapists tend to be unsavory in most facets of their life, but—forget Ben for a moment—the real issue is what we're going to do about my mother and the Washington Post reporter."

Cagey Martin was back and he glared at me from across the room with his hands on his hips. "What do you want me to do?"

I heaved another big sigh and admitted, "I don't know. This is why I need your help. I need you to help me figure out how to make this right."

He shrugged, his tone growing distant. "Make what right? I don't see the problem."

This gave me pause because I felt like the problem was obvious. Giving him the benefit of the doubt, I decided to spell it out for him. "The problem, Martin, is that your father is using our involvement with each other—"

"We're not *involved*. You're my girlfriend."

"He is using our relationship to discredit my mother. He's already given two interviews where he alluded that she is softening on the Net Neutrality bill because of me, because we're dating."

"So?"

My eyes widened at his flippant response and I was struck slightly speechless; I parroted, "So…? So? So, this is very bad. We need to make him stop."

"It's none of our business." Martin scratched his chin, sounding aloof, and shrugged again.

I was really beginning to dislike his shrugs.

I was also starting to lose my temper.

What the hell?

I stood from the bed and paced, ranting to all four walls. "Of course it's our business. It's everybody's business. Net neutrality is *everyone's* business! Just because you've never had to work for anything in your life doesn't mean it's not your business."

Martin's expression grew stony and fierce, his jaw set. I regretted the words as soon as I'd said them.

"Okay, sorry." I reached my hands out between us then let them fall to my sides when he continued to glare at me. "I didn't mean that how it sounded. But you don't get to ignore important issues that affect everyone but the top one percent just because you're in the top one percent. It's irresponsible."

"What do you suggest that I do?" The question was clearly meant to be equal parts rhetorical and sarcastic. "You've met my father. He's not going to listen to me. He won't listen to anyone. And if I go against him, he'll cut me off."

"Martin, what's left then? Hmm? I can't let my mother step down because of bogus charges. If you can't get him to listen to you then the only other option is…is…" *For us to break up.*

I didn't say it, but I might as well have said it because it was obviously the only remaining option.

Martin immediately grasped my unspoken meaning because his

entire body went rigid and his eyes grew thunderous. His menacing denial was softly spoken.

"No. No fucking way."

"Then give me another solution."

"No, that's bullshit." He charged toward me, but I held my ground as he quietly raged at me. "This has nothing to do with us. You're looking for an excuse. This is just an excuse to shit all over everything we've built. You've been looking for a reason to run away, and this is it."

I reached forward to touch him but he twisted away, stalking back to his dresser and slamming another drawer.

I didn't like the pleading edge that entered my voice, as I said, "No. This is me standing up for what I believe in. Your father is discrediting my mother, damaging her reputation and people are *buying into it*. She has worked her whole life against corruption. She has fought for good and justice and peace and prosperity."

Martin scoffed, his words mocking. "She's not superwoman, Parker."

"She is to me. And I'm not going to do nothing while your dad uses me to make her look like a corrupt flake."

He shook his head, clearly frustrated. "Listen to me. What could you possibly do to make Denver Sandeke change his mind? He never changes his mind. Talking to him is useless. Arguing with him just makes him happy. He gets off on other people's misery."

"We have to stop him."

"We can't."

"So...what? Am I supposed to just let him say these terrible things?"

"What choice do you have?" He turned completely around, finally facing me again and giving nothing away with his expression.

"I'll give an interview. I'll call the reporter from the Washington Post."

"It won't make a difference. We *are* dating. We are together. Our families aren't close, but that doesn't matter because perception is all that matters. Why would anyone believe you over my father? They wouldn't." I saw that he was trying to talk me down from getting my hopes up, and he was trying to be gentle and break the reality of the situation to me, the fruitlessness of it.

But he was wrong, because there was one person that could discredit Denver Sandeke...

"But you *could*."

Martin stared at me, his gaze becoming increasingly calculating and guarded. When he responded his words were measured and slow. "No. I couldn't. Like I said, he'll cut me off, and I am so close. I'll be twenty-one in less than four months. I will not do anything to risk losing access to that money."

"Martin, I could...I could help you. We could move in together, share expenses. You don't need your father's money. You're a freaking genius, and you have all those patents. You don't need his money."

His eyes were now slits and he was shaking his head slowly. "No. You don't understand. My father has forgotten about the trust, and I need that trust. I need those houses. I have plans, I can't just abandon them."

"What plans?" I reached for him but he pulled his hand from my grasp and turned away, so I spoke to his back. "Tell me the plan. What are you talking about?"

He walked to his desk chair; his big, powerful hands gripping the back of it, and gave me his profile. "The venture capitalist deal in New York. The houses all over the world. The sixty million dollars. The satellites. The plan, everything I've been working for to completely screw him over. If I discredit him now then he'll look for ways to make me miserable, and he'll remember the trust. Then I'm cut off and it all goes away."

I stared at the side of his face, my mouth open but no sound emerging, because I was mostly confused. After a moment I found some words. I wasn't sure they were the right ones, but they were the only words I had.

"I'm sorry, I don't understand what you're talking about. What do houses all over the world have to do with sixty million dollars? And how are satellites going to screw over Denver Sandeke?"

Martin exhaled but it sounded like an impatient growl. "The houses, Parker. His houses are all in my name and I am four months away from accessing the trust when I turn twenty-one." Martin faced me, his stance inflexible. "I have buyers for six of them, and I'm confident I'll have buyers for the other eleven soon. That's how I'm getting the sixty million."

I blinked furiously. "You can't do that, those aren't your houses."

"They're in my name."

"But—"

"And, all together, they're worth well over sixty million. And I'm selling them and he doesn't know a goddamn thing about it. And when I've sold them, I'm investing the money into launching telecom satellites that will replace traditional landlines, DSLs, and—in some cases —fiber optic cable. I'm going to break the telecom monopolies that Sandeke Telecom holds. I'm going to give the people in his service areas an alternative source for their Internet and phone. I'm going to drive my father out of business and make billions in the process. But I can't do that if he cuts me off now."

My face scrunched and twisted. This was...this was unbelievable. This was global scale corporate warfare and so beyond my frame of reference.

"It can't, I mean, it can't be as simple as that. If satellites are the answer to the great telecom monopoly debate, then it seems to be that someone else would have solved it by now."

Martin's frown was severe, his eyes cutting, almost mocking. "Have you ever heard of Elon Musk?"

"Yes. Everyone knows who he is."

"Not everyone."

"He's the CEO of Tesla and a genius philanthropist," I supplied blandly.

"Yeah, well look up his work on alternate sources of Internet delivery. It *is* as simple as satellites, but there is nothing simple about these satellites."

I huffed then growled, punching my hands through the air as I fought to control my temper. "Well...so...fine! You have your 'fancy satellite plan'! It's going to work. You'll screw your father and break up his monopoly. Where does that leave us?"

"Right where we are. Nothing between us changes!" He was yelling again.

"What does that even mean?" I was also yelling and appealing to the ceiling, throwing my hands in the air.

"Us. Together. And we ignore my father."

"But we can't. We can't ignore him. If we do nothing, then my mother steps down and her life's work is over."

Martin shrugged, scratched the back of his neck, and said with infuriating ambivalence and granite resolve in his eyes, "Not. My. Problem."

In that moment I wanted to punch him in the face, because I felt like he'd punched me in the stomach. Resentment filled my mouth, choked me as we glared at each other, our rapid-fire argument over and nothing resolved. I was twisting in the wind and he didn't seem to care. To my infinite irritation I felt the first signs of tears—stinging eyes, wobbly chin—and was powerless to fight it.

I couldn't control the shakiness in my voice as I whispered, "I trusted you."

"You *can* trust me." His voice was steady, yet clearly laced with frustration. "I would do anything for you…except this. You can't ask me to do this, to go against him publically, when I'm *so close* to seeing this through."

Again we stared at each other and neither of us gave an inch. I swallowed the building thickness in my throat, creeping despair twisting its fingers around my chest and making each breath painful. Yet I had to give us one more shot. I was trying my best to fight for him, fight for us. I gathered a deep breath and tried once more to appeal to him.

I was careful to keep the volume of my voice low, though I struggled to keep it steady. "If you love me…" He closed his eyes with a slow blink and he turned slightly away. Martin shook his head, stared at the floor, with his jaw set, and his powerful arms once more crossed over his chest. "If you love me then it *is* your problem, because I can't let my mother do that. I can't let her step down because of me and my choices."

"There is nothing you can do, Kaitlyn." His tone was flat and entirely patronizing.

And he was wrong.

There was one thing I could do, one finite solution that would solve the problem, but that was also going to break my heart. I felt a new, more powerful wave of tears build behind my eyes as I stared at his outward expression of indifference.

A single thought bubbled to the surface of my mind: *he's betrayed me.*

I'd flung myself off a cliff, trusting that he'd be there to catch me, but he let me fall. I hadn't realized until that moment how completely I'd trusted him. I was so stupid.

I felt my heart slow and sputter, thump and crack. The dam broke and gave way to a flood of bitter tears.

I mimicked his stance, crossed my arms over my chest and lifted my chin, hoping the posturing would give me the bravery I needed even as fat drops of saltwater spilled from my eyes.

"You're wrong, Martin. There is something I can do."

Martin became very still, quiet. His eyes cut to mine and they were sharp, focused.

"I'm breaking up with you." I made no move to wipe away the wet tracks because…what was the point?

"Kaitlyn." My name sounded like a plea and an accusation. I firmed my jaw. He shook his head. "Don't say that."

"What other choice do I have?" I was screaming at him, my anger reaching a boiling point. "If we break up then this goes away, there is no bias because we're not together."

"But we'd…what?" He searched my face. "We'd see each other in secret?"

I stubbornly shook my head, feeling the physical effects of misery. Yet grim, soothing resolve crept its way up my spine, wrapping my heart and mind in a blanket of numb certainty. He must've seen something shift, some change in my expression, because he rushed forward and gripped my arms.

"No...no, no, no. That's not going to happen. You are not doing this."

I released a pained breath that sounded more like a sob and looked at the wall over his shoulder, sniffling. Tears fell freely and I barely felt the cold trails they left on my cheeks. This desolation was like bee stings on every surface of my skin, my stomach rolling and clenching. I felt like I was being torn apart.

When I responded, it was without emotion, because I already knew what his answer would be. "I don't think I really have a choice here, unless you can think of another solution."

"You're just going to give up? Just like that?"

I twisted out of his grip, walking backward several steps, and spat at him, "You make it sound like this is easy for me. This isn't easy. You won't give up your fancy satellite plans and I can't let my mother suffer because of your father's lies. You're asking me to choose between right and wrong. I have to choose right."

"That's bullshit!" I winced because his voice was loud and severe, his eyes flashing, his expression livid as he closed the distance between us and jabbed his finger in my face. "If you don't want to be with me then own it. Don't blame it on some higher cause. You own it!"

"I do want to be with you! I lo—" I turned, covered my face before he could see it crumple, and walked three steps away, biting my tongue.

This was madness. I thought we loved each other, and yet...

Reason reared its affable head and politely suggested that one does not fall in love with a person over the course of a week. What I was feeling was the infatuation of newness; it was his smile and the way he touched me and the way he looked at me.

Love was lasting. Love finds a way. Love endures.

But we'd had a week. One week. Only a week.

"A beautiful week," I said through my tears, not immediately realizing I'd spoken out loud.

"What?"

"We had a beautiful week," I whispered, as I finally wiped the wetness from my face and dropped my hands, reason reminding me that just because I didn't feel calm, didn't mean I couldn't be calm.

I would be calm.

I would not be hysterical.

I would walk out of this room, walk away from him, and never second-guess the decision, because it was the right thing to do.

Therefore, I lifted my chin, mentally preparing myself for what came next, and dug deep for courage. "I'll always remember it. I'll always…think of you."

My vision blurred again. I needed to leave before more tears fell, because once I really started, it was going to be an epic sob fest. Multiple boxes of tissues were going to be used.

He spoke through clenched teeth; I knew he was furious, but he also sounded desperate. "I swear to God, Parker, if you leave, if you do this then that's it. I swear, I'm done. I can't forever be trying to prove to you that what I feel for you, what I want from you is real."

"I believe you," I said without turning around. I couldn't look at him. I needed to leave. I wrapped my arms around my middle and after a short pause, walked to the door.

"Don't," he said quietly, his voice roughened with an edge of desperation. "Now I am begging, please don't do this. I love you." He exhaled this last part, the last word ending abruptly like he'd swallowed it, like it'd cost him.

A shock passed though me, his words were physical, possessed the ability to electrify the air, reach out to me, into my chest and squeeze my numbed heart. My steps faltered, my shoulders curved forward, and my arms held me tighter. I felt as though I was holding myself together. If I moved my hands I might shatter to pieces.

I turned, tried to gather a deep breath but found I couldn't, the pain was too sharp, too acute. I met his gaze directly; the force of it, the pleading and prideful ferocity nearly knocked me over.

"Then help me," I begged in return. "Please help me find another way. I don't want to do this. Help me fight your father."

His eyes were despairing, tortured as they moved over my face. He pleaded, "We can see each other in secret."

"No. Someone would find out, and then it would make my mother look even worse."

"He will cut me off, Parker." Martin shook his head, pain and frustration and helplessness casting a contorting shadow over his features. "I can't go against him, not yet."

I released the breath I'd been holding. My voice was watery but firm. I shrugged, then said, "Then…I guess this is goodbye."

[14]

ATOMIC WEIGHTS

I COULDN'T STOP crying.

I just physically could not.

I hurt. I hurt so completely. And every time I closed my eyes I saw his face and I hurt more. I was choking on it, asphyxiating, drowning in it.

I was not this person, or at least, I'd never been this person before right now. I was calm and detached; I abhorred drama. I never understood girls who cried about boys. But I did now. I totally freaking got it. I had no control over this agony, I had no choice but to feel it, all of it, and it sucked.

So I buried myself under my covers and cried like it was my job and I was hoping for a promotion. I cried until my pillow was soaked and the only thing that came close to the hurt in my heart was the throbbing in my head.

And this is how Sam found me that night after breaking up with Martin.

She paused when she opened the door to our room, the light from the suite area spilling across my bed, and I met her eyes as they scanned my splotchy, swollen face. The corners of her mouth turned down as she pressed her lips together.

"Anyone die?" she asked.

I shook my head and pressed my face to the damp pillow, my words muffled, as I responded melodramatically, "No. But I want to."

"You want to die?"

"Yes, I want to die."

"Why?"

"We broke up."

Aaaaand more crying. I hiccupped on a ragged sob.

"Well...shit." I heard her sigh, then say gently as she rubbed my back, "I'll be right back with stuff for ice cream sundaes."

The door clicked shut behind her. So I cried and wrapped myself in the chaotic thoughts that had plagued me since leaving Martin.

Maybe I was being selfish.

Maybe Martin's revenge was more important than my mother's reputation and providing affordable Internet service to millions of people.

Maybe we could see each other in secret and no one would find out.

Maybe we were just taking a break for four months and we'd pick right back up once his master revenge plan was set in motion.

Maybe I was turning into a pathetic creature grasping at straws because I missed him with every cell in my body and the thought of never seeing him or talking to him again made me want to light myself on fire.

Not *actually* light myself on fire, but do something drastic because I just freaking hurt so very, very bad.

And it had only been five hours.

Sam returned sometime later while I was in the middle of replaying my conversation with Martin in my head for the hundredth time and therefore second-guessing my decision for the millionth time.

She flipped on the light, making me groan, wince, and wish more fervently for death.

"Katy, take the pink pills by your bed and drink some water. You're probably dehydrated."

"What's in the pink pills?"

"Ibuprofen."

I struggled to sit up, reached for the pills, and started to cry. "Okay," I said through my tears, "I'll take the pills, but nothing will *ever* make me feel good *ever* again."

Sam *tsked* sadly and I heard the clatter of dishes and spoons, the rustling of a plastic bag, and the sure sounds of an ice cream sundae being prepared. After I finished taking a gulp of water and Sam tossed me a new box of tissues, she placed the bowl in my hands.

"Eat your ice cream and tell me what happened."

I shrugged, squinted at the mint chocolate chip and fudge in my bowl. "I don't know what to say."

"Do I need to hire a hit man?"

I took a bite. It tasted good. I was numbly amazed that anything could possibly taste good. "No. I broke up with him."

"You broke up with him?"

I nodded, pushing the ice cream to one side so I could get a spoonful of fudge.

"Does this have something to do with your mom?"

I nodded again, my throat tight. Suddenly I didn't want fudge because fudge wasn't Martin, and fudge would never be Martin.

Stupid fudge.

Holding her own bowl, Sam insinuated herself next to me on the bed and wrapped an arm around my shoulders. "Kaitlyn, tell me everything. Talk to me. Let me help."

"Nothing will help." I knew I sounded emo and morose but I didn't care. Being dramatic was the only thing that felt right.

"Then tell me because I'm nosey. Tell me what happened."

So I did. I told her all about Martin's pariah parents and how he'd grown up being used and humiliated—though I didn't share the specifics—and about the impossible situation with my mother, and a vague description of Martin's plans for revenge.

It took me an hour because I had to stop every once in a while to sob like an infant. Talking about it was reliving it again and I experienced fresh pain with each word. However, when I was finished, when my tale of woe was complete, I felt somehow different.

I didn't feel better. I just felt less…despairing.

Despairing, desolate, dejected, depressed, hopeless, inconsolable, miserable…

"I'm sorry if this makes things weird with you and Eric." I said this to my melted bowl of ice cream because it hurt to lift my eyeballs.

"What do you mean?"

"I'm just saying, I hope this doesn't put you or Eric in an awkward situation. You shouldn't let my break up with Martin affect your relationship."

She was quiet for a moment, and I felt her eyes on me. "Kaitlyn… Eric and I aren't in a relationship."

Even though it hurt, I lifted my scratchy eyes to her, knew my face betrayed my confusion. "You're not?"

"No, hon. We're not dating."

"Then…then what happened last week?" My voice was nasally and a little squeaky.

She shrugged. "Nothing of significance. I mean, yeah…we had a good time together, but we're not dating."

"Did you sleep with him?" I didn't know I was going to ask the question before I asked the question, and I winced because it was rude, and sounded judgmental and demanding.

Her half smile was just north of being patronizing. "Yes. We slept together. And we hung out and made out and had a lot of fun. I like him a lot, but I'm not looking for a relationship and I told him that at the beginning of the week. Between school and tennis and now needing a summer job, I was looking for a good time. So we had a good time, but I doubt I'll see him again."

New tears flooded my eyes and I blinked them away, tangentially amazed that I could still cry. "Am I a bad feminist? You can tell me the truth."

"What are you talking about?" Sam chuckled and tried to untangle a patch of my hair near my ear.

"Because I fell in love with Martin. I started falling in love with him the moment he kissed me in the chemistry lab. I am totally weak for him. And the thought of sleeping with someone without being in love…I don't know. It makes me want to throw up."

"Kaitlyn, you and I are two completely different people with completely different temperaments, experiences, and personalities. Not all women can—or should—have casual sex. Just like, believe it or not, not all men can have casual sex. And your inability to have sex without deeper feelings doesn't make you a bad feminist any more than my love for lace panties and the color pink makes me a bad feminist. Do you see what I mean?"

I nodded, still feeling like a bad feminist. But more than that, I still hurt. The absence of Martin screamed in my ears and the acute pain of sudden loss tortured my soul…*ugh!* Now I was contemplating my tortured soul. I was pathetic.

I groaned. "What is wrong with me? How can I be this upset over a guy I was with technically less than a week?"

"First of all, stop beating yourself up for what you're feeling."

"I'm pathetic. I'm a drama llama. I'm *that* girl. I've spent years judging that girl, and now I'm her and I feel so terrible for judging her because, if she felt one tenth of the agony I feel right now, then I need to write her an apology letter. I should punch myself in the face for being so judgey."

"Kaitlyn, we are all *that* girl sooner or later. You can't know or understand another person's pain until you've lived through a similar experience. You fell hard and you fell fast. It was dating boot camp on that island, and you were all in. Girl, you just lost your virginity two days ago! Give yourself some time to adjust."

"Oh, Sam, how am I going to make it through the rest of my life when almost six hours post breakup I'm already contemplating death by fire as a preferable alternative to the ache in my heart?"

Sam sighed and wrapped her arms around me. She laid her head on my shoulder and said softly, "Kaitlyn, stop and think about this, really, really think about what's going on. Think about what you know about this guy."

"I know he loves me and I broke up with him and I don't even really know why."

"You know why. You broke up with him because he was unwilling to do the right thing."

"But he loves me and—"

She made a sound in the back of her throat that reminded me of Marge from the Simpsons and interrupted my whiny tirade. "Here is the truth, and I'm sorry if it hurts, but here it is: Martin is never going to choose anyone—even you—over himself."

I winced because... *Gah, right in the feels.*

I pressed a damp tissue to my face. "Gee, thanks."

"I'm not saying this to be hurtful. You are beautiful and amazing and so smart." Sam paired this with a squeeze. "And did I mention beautiful? But the thing is..." she lifted her head and searched my face, "the thing is, he doesn't know how to love. He doesn't. You said it yourself, his parents are pariahs. He knows all about self-preservation, and he's thinking only of revenge. He's the Count of Monte Cristo."

I gave a pitiful laugh and shook my head. "I know you're trying to help, but you don't know him like I do. I *know* he loves me."

"I'm sure, on some level, in Martin's universe of one, he's willing to make room for you. I'm sure he does love you, as much as he's capable. But, that's just it. It's a universe of one, and giving you a corner isn't what you deserve. You deserve a universe of two, and a pedestal, and cabana boys to peel your grapes."

Tears squeezed out of my eyes even as I snorted. I wiped them away with my tissue, which was basically just lint at this point.

"I don't want cabana boys. I just want...I want..." I glanced at the ceiling and shook my head.

"I know. You want Martin Sandeke to choose you over his master-mind revenge plot, a revenge plot that's occupied his mind since he was a teenager and toward which he's been working since he reached the age of reason."

I nodded and added sarcastically, "Yes. Exactly. Why can't I be more important to him than a life-time ambition?"

Sam wasn't at all sarcastic when she squeezed my hand and said, "But don't you see? You *should* be. You're not asking him to do anything wrong or illegal, you're not asking him to choose you over his convictions. You're asking him to do the right thing, the good thing, the honorable thing. If he really loved you, really and truly loved you, then *you* would be more important to him than revenge."

I stared at her until she grew blurry in my vision and added absent-mindedly, "But I'm not."

"But you're not," she echoed, giving me a sad face, then pulled me into a hug, whispering again my ear, "And you should be."

* * *

I TEXTED MY mother on Monday and told her that Martin and I broke up. She texted me back that she would arrange through the chemistry department for me to finish my lab credits without a lab partner. She also said she was looking forward to seeing me over summer break.

When I received nothing else from her—no call to ask how I was, no thank you or recognition of what the break up cost me—I became irrationally angry and played 'Killing in the Name' by Rage Against the Machine on my acoustic guitar until 2:37 a.m. I only stopped because Sam came home from a late night study session and needed sleep. When she left the next morning, I picked up my guitar and played it again.

But playing angry music on an acoustic guitar is completely dissat-isfying, so I stopped. What I needed were drums.

The next week was really strange. Sam said I was in mourning, but somehow I felt like the one who was dead. Life became mostly periods of calm detachment infrequently interrupted by flashes of intense and painful chaos.

Toward the end of this endless week of insignificant moments, I wondered why anyone would want to fall in love. Falling in love sucked—figuratively, it sucked the life out of me, left me hollow, a desolate wasteland of suckage.

Except when I played my guitar.

So I played my guitar, but instead of playing angry music, I played guitar suites—mostly classical—but somehow made them sound angry.

I also ignored George's messages about the Sunday family agenda. As well I skipped the Sunday call, though I did give my cell phone the double finger salute when it rang. Then I played my guitar.

On the Monday one week after the break up, I was a hot mess. I hadn't been showering...much. But I took comfort in small accomplishments, like brushing my teeth once a day and making it to my classes.

Going to class gave me something to focus on. As well, before my vector calculus class, I received a huge shock when I overheard that someone in Martin's fraternity had been kicked out of school and arrested for attempted rape and assault of a minor.

"Who?" I asked loudly, not caring that this question would label me as an unabashed eavesdropper.

The two guys glanced over their shoulders at me, apparently found me harmless in my sweatpants, tangled hair, and stained Lord of the Rings T-shirt, then turned toward me so I could be included in the conversation.

The ginger spoke first. "One of the crew guys, Salsmar. His picture is in the paper if you really want to know and there's supposed to be a video. They're not releasing the name of the girl 'cause turns out she's underage."

Benjamin Salsmar. Ben. Ben the rapist.

Oh my God!

My stomach dropped. I felt like such a terrible person. I should have called the police about Ben as soon as I arrived back on campus. But I'd forgotten and given myself over to personal drama and now someone had suffered because of me.

Ugh...just, ugh!

"Just another fraternity fuckup," the darker-haired boy said derisively. "It would be news if this kind of shit didn't happen all the time. Show me a fraternity guy who doesn't rape girls, that would be a shocker."

"Yeah," the ginger nodded, adding, "it'll be newsworthy if Salsmar actually gets convicted. Usually these guys get a bailout from their daddy and a slap on the wrist."

"But with the video?" I pressed. "If they have a video, then surely he'll see some jail time?"

They both shrugged, like power, money, and influence mattered more than hard and tangible evidence. Then class started and our impromptu gossip fest was over.

But I couldn't focus on class because I had ants in my pants. I was sure Martin had orchestrated Ben's arrest, or at least had been responsible for making sure it was caught on tape.

* * *

By the end of the third week after the breakup, I was showering semi-daily and I hadn't cried in seven days. I'd also lost fifteen pounds...not even cookies could hold my interest. I hadn't returned any of my mother's calls, nor had I participated in Sunday family meetings.

I was once again hiding in closets. After class I would walk back to my dorm, step into my closet, and shut the door. Sometimes I would bring my guitar and play my own compositions and improvisations. All the songs were morose.

I hadn't seen or heard from Martin and everything still hurt. His absence was everywhere. Therefore, sitting in the darkness and enjoying the lack of sensation, the lack of feeling was a relief.

I was not getting better; things weren't getting easier. Life was various levels of *blah* and horrifically painful.

As such, things went from blah to horrifically painful in the middle of the afternoon on Thursday. I was walking home intent on spending some quality time in the blackness of my closet when I saw him.

My feet stopped moving on their own, and I told myself not to blink or breathe, just in case he was a mirage. I didn't realize until that moment how hungry I was for a glimpse of him. Even though it hurt to the depths of my melodramatic and tortured soul, I stared at Martin.

He was sitting in the student union at a circular table. His big hands were in his hair and he was studying papers on the table before him. Next to Martin sat a very pretty blonde in a grey business suit, a black leather attaché case on the chair next to her. I noted that she looked about ten or so years older than me, but I wondered how much of that was the suit and makeup and air of professionalism.

Meanwhile he looked just the same. His hair was a little messy, but that was probably because he'd been pulling his fingers through it. But his color was fine. He looked fine. He looked perfectly fine.

I forced myself to take a breath and move to the wall, out of the flow of pedestrian traffic. My brain re-booted after close to a minute of standing and staring like a crazy person at my...at my Martin.

But he wasn't my Martin.

A fresh wave of pain pierced my chest and I struggled to inhale. It felt like someone had stabbed me, right through the heart. Every beat was a sluggish ache.

He wasn't *my* anything. And he looked perfectly fine. He was fine and I was a mess because he'd never loved me and I'd allowed myself to fall completely in love with him...like a complete idiot.

Cold certainty and acceptance was a bitter but necessary salve to the open wound I'd been carrying around. It was just as Sam said: he wasn't capable of love. I was wasting my time, both staring at him now and pining for him over the last three weeks. Everything about my time with Martin Sandeke had been a waste of time.

A truly desolate yet comforting numbness wrapped around me like a blanket. I embraced it. Hell, I slathered myself in it and wanted to have its babies. It was armor and a weapon, and finally, finally a tool to combat feeling like an exposed nerve. I was so tired of being vulnerable and helpless.

At last, after indulging myself with one more look—noting with calm detachment that he was now smiling at the woman, and she was laughing at something he'd said—I shook my head to clear it of his image and turned away.

I hadn't smiled in over three weeks. But I hadn't cried in seven days and I wasn't going to cry today. Furthermore, I decided I was never going to cry over Martin Sandeke again.

I decided to take the long way through the student union building rather than walk within feet of his table. The long way took me by a cluster of vending machines, so I stopped and decided to grab a bottle of Dr. Pepper and some peanut M&M's. I couldn't actually remember the last time I'd eaten and that was completely unacceptable. I loved food and I'd allowed Martin-anguish to eclipse every facet of my life.

I was putting a stop to his joy-sucking right now and I was going to use the magic of food to do it.

I fished two crisp dollar bills from my wallet and had just claimed my lunch of champions when I felt a hand on my shoulder.

I glanced at the owner, expecting to find a fellow student asking for change. Instead my eyes connected with Martin's. I was surprised, but so completely numb at this point that I'm sure my expression betrayed nothing but indifference.

I did note that he looked great. Really, really great. Beautiful even. He glowed, like he always had. He was dressed in a black T-shirt, the graphic image on the front depicted some rowing scene, and dark jeans. I noted that he never wore skinny jeans; this was probably because his thighs were too muscular and skinny jeans were for skinny guys. He would never be skinny.

Granted, his expression wasn't happy, but he didn't look like he'd been suffering. He wasn't fifteen pounds lighter and white as a sheet. His eyes weren't bloodshot. His hands weren't shaking. He appeared to be angry but nowhere near heartbroken, at least not the version I saw in the mirror every morning.

I felt like throwing up.

Averting my eyes, I tried to step around him, but he countered and halted my progress.

He moved as though he were going to grab my wrist so I stopped and yanked my arm out of his reach, rocking backward. Since I was basically trapped in the vending machine alcove, I turned my face to the side, inspected the wall, and gave him my profile.

At length he asked, "Will you look at me?"

I tensed. Hearing his voice did something terrible. It broke through this new barrier, the detachment I'd embraced. Therefore I didn't want to look at him again. I was finally exhibiting control over my feelings and I couldn't take the chance. I suspected looking at him now would hurt like a motherfucker.

And apparently, in addition to discovering that just seeing someone can cause physical pain and illness, I was discovering the cathartic and necessary nature of curse words. Despite my expansive vocabulary, there existed no other way to describe how much it would hurt to look at Martin.

In my peripheral vision I sensed movement and I flinched away before he could touch me. I crossed my arms over my chest.

"Goddammit," he seethed. His anger and frustration settled over us, a dark, accusatory fog.

We stood like that for a minute and I imagined I was building an actual wall of bricks between us. I'd volunteered for three summers during high school with Habitat for Humanity and I could build a heckofa brick wall.

He broke the stalemate. "Talk to me, Parker."

I shook my head and closed my eyes, pressing my lips together in a firm line. Despite the sounds of college life around us I could hear him breathe. He wasn't breathing loudly, it's just I could hear it. And it reminded me of the times he'd held me on the boat. I pushed that thought from my mind before it made me cry—because it would make me cry—and turned my attention back to the fictional brick wall.

"You look like shit," he said.

Yeah, it was a crappy thing to say. But it was so Martin. So thoughtless and candid. I did look like shit. And I realized that Martin wasn't a very nice person, not even to me. He was honest first and foremost; sometimes his honesty meant he said nice things to me. But he was never nice for the sake of being nice, or polite because he wanted to spare my feelings. Not once.

I wondered if it even occurred to him that I had feelings...

"Have you been eating?" He shuffled a step forward, his tone nonchalant, almost friendly. "You need a sandwich, let me buy you lunch."

I opened my eyes, affixed them to the floor, but remained silent. Seeing him had satisfied some fundamental—and likely unhealthy—need to witness how he was dealing with the breakup. Was he as tortured and ruined as me? I had my answer and now I couldn't wait to never see him again.

Unexpectedly he blurted, "If you don't talk to me I'll go crazy."

His words were quiet but rough, as though torn from his chest. They certainly had the effect of tearing at my chest. Searing pain flared in my stomach and I had to count to ten before I could breathe again.

I said nothing. Had this happened before today, had he approached me even one hour earlier, I likely would have burst into tears and begged him to take me back. But, for better or for worse, seeing him moments ago looking so well had flipped my off switch. I'd finally accepted we were over—mostly due to the fact that we never truly were.

"I love you." He exhaled the words and I almost believed him. He was so close I could feel the breath fall over my face, a whispered caress that pierced my heart and stomach, ripping and shredding. He repeated, "I love you."

Then he touched me, his hands cupping my face.

"Don't." I tried to jerk my head away but he held me tighter, stepping into me and backing me against the wall.

I lifted my eyes but couldn't raise them above his neck as he tilted my chin up and pressed his lips to mine. He kissed me. I didn't kiss him back, holding onto my earlier resolve and numbness like a lifeline. His forehead fell against mine and he held me there, breathing my air.

"Please talk to me. Please."

"There is nothing to say." I was gratified by the hollow quality and steadiness of my voice.

"I need you."

I shook my head in denial, because I knew he didn't. If he needed me then he wouldn't have let me go, he would have chosen us over revenge. If he needed me then he wouldn't have been able to smile at pretty blondes and look exactly the same as he had three weeks ago after a vacation in the Caribbean.

"You need to leave me alone," I responded through clenched teeth.

"I can't." He pressed his lips to mine again, taking another kiss, lingering there like he was afraid to move, like it would be the last time. He spoke against my mouth. "I can't leave you alone. It's been almost a month and you're all I think about."

"That's a lie."

"No, goddamn you, it isn't! Haven't you noticed me following you? Haven't you seen me outside your dorm, waiting for you? Fucking hell, Parker, you *never* see me, you never have, but that doesn't mean I'm not there."

I gripped his wrists and pulled his hands from my face, twisting away and seeking to put distance between us. His words were confusing because I did see him, just moments ago, smiling at someone else and appearing completely fine. I didn't want his words. I didn't want anything from him.

Despite my certainty and earlier pledge, I felt the beginning of a chin wobble and a stinging moisture behind my eyes. "If I'm all you think about then are you ready to tell the world your father is an evil asshole and being with me is not an alliance between our families?"

This was met with silence and the silence fed my detachment.

I huffed a humorless laugh. "Yeah, I thought so."

"Kaitlyn, there is no reason why we can't be together in secret, if you would only—"

It was the same argument; nothing had changed, so I interrupted him. "If we're seen together then all of this has been pointless. My mother—"

"Fuck your mother," he growled.

I winced, stared at the floor because I didn't want to see him, and when I spoke my voice was unsteady. "This is pointless. You need to let me go."

"What if I can't? Hmm? What if I don't? What if I call the Washington Post and tell the reporter that we're still together, that our families are closer than ever?"

I finally lifted my eyes to his so he could see how serious I was, and that—in that moment—I hated him a little. I looked at him even though it hurt like a motherfucker.

Somehow I managed to say, "That's blackmail."

"If that's what it takes." He punctuated this with a belligerent shrug.

I shook my head, mostly at myself for thinking we were ever a team. "Martin, there's a time to fight, and there is a time to bow out gracefully."

"You never fight," he spat, his mouth twisted in an unattractive sneer, his eyes dark blue flames.

I fleetingly thought of how I'd fought for him in front of his father, how I'd fought for him and for us in his room three weeks ago. But what was the point? Arguing would get us nowhere. *We* didn't exist.

Instead I said, "What do you want me to do? Do you want me to blackmail you? Issue threats? Call your father and tell him about your plan to sell his houses?"

He winced like I'd struck him, blinking several times in rapid succession. "You wouldn't do that."

"No. I wouldn't. I respect your decision, even if I think it's a mistake."

"So you bow out gracefully, like a coward."

"You're wrong. You're so wrong. I'm fighting for what I believe in, I'm going to do the right thing—"

"Self-sacrificing, martyring bullshit!'

"—and I'm not going to change my mind. So it's time for you to find the self-control to bow out gracefully and let me go."

Eyes flashing, Martin shifted on his feet, his stance telling me he was preparing to launch another verbal volley, so I quickly added, allowing a hint of pleading in my voice, letting it waver and shake, "If you ever had the slightest feeling for me, you will respect my decision. You will walk away right now and you will leave me alone. I need you to *leave me alone*. You are ruining me."

His blue-green eyes were glassy and raw with pain as they searched mine. I recognized his hurt because it was an echo of the suffocating agony I'd been carrying with me every day.

After a long moment he nodded once, his mouth a flat line. His eyes fell away, searching but not looking at any one thing. I saw his chest rise and fall, heard the end of an unsteady exhale, before he turned and left.

His stride (as expected) was confident as always. Every step of his smooth gait just proved that Sam had been right. He was a universe of one and I wasn't enough.

I watched him go, watched the back of his head until he turned a corner.

Then I ran home. I sat in my dark closet. And I cried.

~END PART 2~

ABOUT THE AUTHOR

Penny Reid lives in Seattle, Washington with her husband, three kids, and an inordinate amount of yarn. She used to spend her days writing federal grant proposals as a biomedical researcher, but now she just writes books.

As of 2018, Penny has published 16 novels.

Come find me-
Mailing list signup: http://pennyreid.ninja/newsletter/ (get exclusive stories, sneak peeks, and pictures of cats knitting hats)
Facebook: http://www.facebook.com/PennyReidWriter
Instagram: https://www.instagram.com/reidromance/
Goodreads: http://www.goodreads.com/ReidRomance
Email: pennreid@gmail.com …hey, you! Email me ;-)
Blog: http://pennyreid.ninja
Twitter: https://twitter.com/ReidRomance
Ravelry: http://www.ravelry.com/people/ReidRomance (if you crochet or knit…!)

Read on for:
Penny Reid Book List

Hypothesis Series

(New Adult Romantic Comedy)

Elements of Chemistry: ATTRACTION, HEAT, and CAPTURE (#1)

Laws of Physics: MOTION, SPACE, and TIME (#2, coming 2018)

Fundamentals of Biology: STRUCTURE, EVOLUTION, and GROWTH (#3, coming 2019)

Irish Players (Rugby) Series – by L.H. Cosway and Penny Reid

(Contemporary Sports Romance)

The Hooker and the Hermit (#1)

The Pixie and the Player (#2)

The Cad and the Co-ed (#3)

The Varlet and the Voyeur (#4)

Dear Professor Series

(New Adult Romantic Comedy)

Kissing Tolstoy (#1)

Kissing Galileo (#2, coming 2019)

CPSIA information can be obtained
at www.ICGtesting.com
Printed in the USA
LVHW081505010219
606091LV00016B/793/P